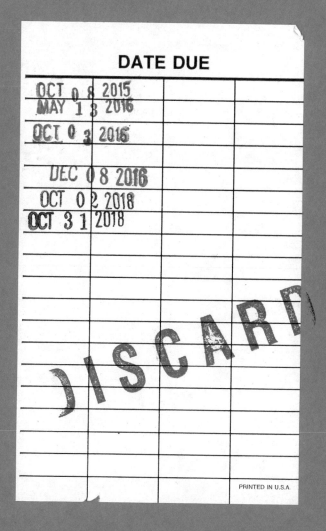

DATE DUE

OCT 0 8 2015			
MAY 1 3 2016			
OCT 0 3 2015			
DEC 0 8 2016			
OCT 0 2 2018			
OCT 3 1 2018			
			PRINTED IN U.S.A.

DISCARD

AGE 14

AGE 14

BY **GEERT SPILLEBEEN**

TRANSLATED BY **TERESE EDELSTEIN**

HOUGHTON MIFFLIN

HOUGHTON MIFFLIN HARCOURT BOSTON NEW YORK 2009

Copyright © 2000 by Geert Spillebeen

First American edition 2009

Originally published in Belgium in 2000 by Averbode

English translation by Terese Edelstein copyright © 2009

by Houghton Mifflin Harcourt Publishing Company

Houghton Mifflin is an imprint of Houghton Mifflin Harcourt Publishing Company.

www.hmhbooks.com

The text of this book is set in Dante MT.

Library of Congress Cataloging-in-Publication Data is on file.

ISBN 978-0-547-05342-4

Manufactured in the United States of America

MP 10 9 8 7 6 5 4 3 2 1

My thanks to curator Jan Dewilde,
Dominiek Dendooven, and colleagues of the
Documentation Center of In Flanders Fields Museum
(Ypres, Belgium); to World War I expert Robert Missinne
(St.-Juliaan-Langemark, Belgium); to Ann Manhaeve, who
"deciphered" the Gothic German. And special thanks
to Dr. James Stacey (Dungarvan-Waterford, Ireland).

A Son

My son was killed while laughing at some jest. I would I knew
What it was, and it might serve me in a time when jests are few.

—Rudyard Kipling

John Condon groped for a chair. He was in shock. Now he knew for sure that not only was he dead and buried, but someone had even dug him up again . . .

He had already been dead for nine years. At the end of May 1915, he learned of his own death from the British Military Government. Coldly they informed him through a telegram that he was missing "somewhere on the battlefield" and was "presumed dead." It had been an enormous blow for his mother. She thought that her youngest son had been safely playing soldier in an

Irish barrack, certainly not at the front. And what about himself? Strange, but during that time of all-out war, John didn't really want to acknowledge the fact that he was gone, "killed in action" somewhere in Belgium. He had heard countless fellows report this kind of information. Every day the newspaper published a list of missing or dead boys. Occasionally a paragraph would appear about a missing soldier who had returned. Thus the news of his own demise had not actually come as a complete surprise. You learned to live with death during those years. How many comrades had he lost? When the Great War ended in 1918, the population of Waterford consisted primarily of old men. Ireland and all of Great Britain were bursting with young widows and grieving girls.

But today, the blow was a hard one for John Condon, even after all these years. They had finally found his body. With trembling hands he lay the letter down on the table. It had a proper military letterhead, but the contents were much too hastily penned by some bored military clerk. *What a gruesome way to inform me,* he thought. *Almost worse than the Great War itself.* He read the little wad of paper yet again:

Officer i/c

Infantry Record Office

Warwick (IRELAND), 5 January 1924

Dear Sir,

The undernamed article listed below that was found on the body of the late No. 6322, soldier John Condon (Royal Irish Regiment), has been received here. Please inform me if you wish it sent to you or whether it may be destroyed.

Subject in question: "one piece of boot."

I have no record of place of burial, though this information may be obtained by you from The Chairman of the Imperial War Graves Commission, 82 Baker Street, London W.1.

Stamped and addressed envelope enclosed for your reply.

Yours faithfully,

Captain D. Jones

By order of the Colonel,

Office i/c of the Infantry Record Office

So it's true—I'm really dead, thought John Condon. In a daze he shuffled to the kitchen cupboard and pulled out a drawer. The little box was still there. He opened it and examined the two medals inside. "British War and Victory Medal," he read on one. He let the colorful ribbons glide over his shaking palm. "1914–1915 Star" was engraved on the other. John would never forget how odd it had felt to sign for these posthumous decorations when they arrived: *Patrick Condon.* The real Patrick was dead; he had reported to the front as John. Patrick had given his older brother's name because he himself was too young to be a soldier. He died in Flanders a few weeks before his fourteenth birthday. *In Flanders Fields. Where the poppies blow,* John thought. *Perhaps there are poppies growing on my grave. My little brother's grave. Somewhere in Flanders there is a cross or a headstone that bears my name.*

THIRTEEN YEARS EARLIER

1911

WATERFORD, SOUTH IRELAND

Farewell, School Days

"Give that bag here, you little rotter!" Patrick Condon shouted.

With such a voice one could chase blue flies off horse manure, which always lay in piles on the gleaming cobblestones of the back harbor.

It was a young, crazy voice in the crossing, a boy's voice that constantly wavered between soprano and bass. Patrick Condon was obviously in a cheerful mood, for most of the time he would have barely opened his mouth for such a trifle. If he really wanted something, the other ragamuffins stepped aside on their own accord. Patrick stood head and shoulders above everyone and thus looked older than ten. His rough hands were as big as coal shovels and usually just as black. But no one could say for sure whether he had actually thrashed anyone.

"Like a trick that never fails, Patrick Condon's tough as nails!" he roared, but immediately tried to look serious. "You should be ashamed, Rogers! Raising hell for a dozen bruised apples! Where did you steal them from, anyway? Or was O'Sullivan in on it, too?" He waved mightily with one fist, and with his other he swept the bulging sack of fruit above their heads.

"We'll share." Patrick grabbed the stolen booty and threw the apples at the snickering bystanders, one by one. He put two apples into his pocket and threw the last two onto the cobblestones in front of O'Sullivan and Rogers. "And now get out of here!"

The two boys sped away.

"He always has to be the boss. God bless the day he leaves school," whispered O'Sullivan, afraid that Patrick would hear him.

"You can say that again," said Rogers, nudging his friend.

"You don't get it, Rog."

Rogers stopped, frowned, and looked searchingly at O'Sullivan. "You don't mean it?"

"It's true," O'Sullivan answered. "He has a job. But don't ask me what it is or how he got it."

Bewildered, Rogers looked back at Patrick's disappearing silhouette. He saw the broad shoulders against the light of the setting sun and the drawn-out shadow that danced behind him. "Shit collector in Ballybricken," he blurted out all of a sudden.

A few pennies could sometimes be earned by picking up manure at the pig and cattle market of Ballybricken, the district where Patrick Condon lived.

"There's been gossip about it for a while already. His brother John spilled the beans this afternoon." O'Sullivan was chattering away now. "But I didn't get anything more out of him. I'm sure he was afraid that someone would steal the job from Patrick."

"Or that his strong little brother would let him have it," Rogers sneered. "You know what he's like, that Patrick . . ." He winked and punched the air with his fists.

"Actually, he wants to be a soldier."

"Yes, we've known that, Sully. But first let him practice on the pigs!"

They walked on the cobblestones along the River Suir toward home.

***

Patrick Condon marched with his nose in the air. He was in high spirits. The still air above the water made the black hairs on his sturdy forearms stand up. Ropes and pulleys tapped against the sea of masts along the quay. He made this detour whenever possible. The ships in Port Láirge inspired him to dream away. He wanted to sail over the water to the continent someday. To "la douce France," or to Germany, a country that Mr. Baldwin had talked about at school. "Germany is growing dangerously large—it's becoming an industrial state, a glutton that's lying in wait for our crown," his teacher had said.

"What crown?" the slow-witted Jimmy Salt had asked.

Chuckling, Patrick heaved a sigh at the memory.

"What crown? What crown do you think? The English crown, you idiot!" the teacher had barked. "King George the Fifth's crown. What else?"

"Isn't there an Irish crown, then?" Salty asked. His blubbery face looked puzzled. "Daddy says that the English king makes lots of promises to us Irish but that there—"

"Enough!" Mr. Baldwin roared. "Math lesson! Condon, come to the board!"

"Stupid schoolteacher," Patrick thought good-humoredly now as he walked briskly along. "I'm finally rid of that yapping goody-goody!"

The dark, low tones of an ocean steamer caught Patrick's attention. It sailed out of the inlet, leaving a long white plume behind it. Perhaps it was going to America. He thought about Paddy Stone, a boy from his street who, like so many others, had left for the promised land. Patrick wanted to cross the ocean someday, too.

He turned onto Wheelbarrow Lane. The common man in Waterford thought that was a better name than the official one, the overly chic Thomas's Avenue. Patrick's street wasn't wide enough to be considered an avenue by anyone's standards, certainly not by those who had to pass through with a handcart or a cattle wagon.

He approached the low brick house at number two and opened the door. He could tell he was home by the smell. His mother had a pot of mutton stew on the fire.

Mollie, the wife of his oldest brother, Peter, sat in a corner, nursing her newborn baby. They lived in the little house, too. Mollie turned away, embarrassed.

"Ready for the big day tomorrow?" called his mother, glancing at him.

Patrick bent forward to pass through the doorway. His broad shoulders blocked the outside light. "Yup!" was his curt reply.

Farewell, Childhood

Patrick was out of bed at four in the morning. He hadn't slept a wink. He rubbed his eyes as he carefully unbolted the front door. He had to hurry over the cobblestones to keep up with his father and two brothers. The first horse carts, laden with pigs, were already rattling through the streets of Ballybricken, right on time for the market. Four shadows of various sizes, with hunched shoulders and caps draped over one ear, walked on the other side of the street toward the Waterford harbor. On the way the Condons had to continually step aside to avoid the small herds of cows being driven in their direction by black-smocked men wielding large sticks. Now and then Patrick saw in the half darkness a rough-looking face illuminated by the glow of a cigarette. The rank smell of fresh cow dung penetrated his cold nose. Gradually he found the rhythm for keeping pace with the other three. After ten minutes, his oldest brother turned left toward O'Sullivan's Brewery, where he had found work.

"Bye!" Peter was barely audible.

"See you tonight?" Patrick shouted. Peter didn't answer.

They walked past the back harbor and followed the Suir downriver, toward Port Láirge. Port Láirge, the Celtic name for the Waterford seaport, was the term used by every Irishman. Patrick was familiar with this area along the river. In his mind he could see a few kilometers farther to the magnificent convergence of the Three Sisters: the rivers Suir, Barrow, and Nore. During his summer holidays he had often romped on the fertile green slopes. He knew that just beyond them lay the bay, then the St. George's Channel and the Irish Sea.

Three sisters, thought Patrick. *Two sisters are enough for me. But now there's Mollie and the baby. They're still sleeping, and so is Mother.* He wondered what his first day of work would be like. He would show them what he could do with his hands, at any rate. Better that than being in the schoolroom, hearing the unbearable yammering of those brats in Mr. Baldwin's class.

Far behind them the clock-tower chimes of the Holy Trinity interrupted his thoughts. Four thirty. Ten seconds later the Protestant Christ Church Cathedral chimed, too. Patrick could unerringly distinguish between the sounds of the two clocks, but now he thought they sounded different than usual, one here in the dark and one so far across the water.

"You'll keep your trap shut when I'm with you, understand?" Father broke the silence. The rough voice indicated that he was in a foul mood.

"Yes."

"You're fourteen when I'm not there with you. Got it?"

"But, Pa," John protested. "Patrick is ten—"

"From now on Patrick is fourteen. See? Or do you want to get him fired right away? We can use those few pennies he'll earn."

"Yes, Pa."

Archibald Hook was an enormous plum pudding of a man, with three hairy rolls of blubber around his bull-neck. He held up his immense trousers with a rope that ran between the folds of fat on his tremendous belly. His nickname, "Fatso," was well deserved. But the worst thing was his rancid odor. His hair hung in strings that stuck to his tiny skull and disappeared behind his ears. Even in the morning he sweated so profusely that it seemed as though he had smeared his entire body with a smelly hair tonic.

"This is him, Archie. My youngest son." The friendliness in Father's voice seemed exaggerated.

Patrick knew that Pa was groveling before this monster. The boy looked directly into Archibald Hook's face.

"Name?" the big man growled.

"Patrick," answered his father. "And Condon, just like me. And—"

"How old are you, boy?"

Patrick held his tongue. Even in the morning darkness he could see the blood vessels pulsing through the man's eyes. And that breath—a mix of garlic and gin—was enough to make him gag.

"He just turned fourteen!" Father hastened to say. "So it's no problem, is it, Archie?"

"That remains to be seen," Mr. Hook snapped. "Little blokes *are* problems. You know that from experience." He dabbed his forehead with a gray rag and pointed to the *Caesar,* an empty steamship that towered above the quay. "He can go sweep the hold right away. Peanuts—that'll keep him busy."

Peanuts. *That's a good beginning* flashed through Patrick's head. *Maybe I can start up a business from this. As long as I don't come across that monkey face of Archie the Fatso too often.*

"Okay, thanks, Archie," said Father, and he turned to Patrick. "Let's go, boy." He winked at his other son to follow him.

"Just a moment, Condon!" The giant planted a filthy claw onto Father's shoulder. "Cash in hand!" he growled. "For the first week the boy works for me. After that I get ten percent of his wages."

Dirty swindler, thought Patrick with a shudder. *I barely know this fellow, but he's already making me sick.*

"One day's work for free is what you said, Archie," his father protested. "That was the agreement, wasn't it?"

"And today I want a whole week," the fat man snickered. "But all right, Condon." He turned to a group of boys a bit farther up. "There's no end of candidates, I tell you . . ."

"Fine." Father hesitated. "A week, then."

"And payment in advance, Condon. Now!" Mr. Hook tightened his grip. Patrick looked about and exchanged glances with John, who was looking around as well. The lowlifes at the scene felt a fight coming on and were sizing up the situation. Patrick knew that his father would have absolutely no trouble shaking off Mr. Hook. But the big man had power—the power to rob a person blind.

Father snatched a few coins from his pocket and counted them in his hand. "I can't give you any more now—you know that."

"Bring the rest tomorrow morning straightaway; otherwise Port Láirge will be too small for the both of us!" Mr. Hook roared.

We'll see about that, thought Patrick. He was seething.

Monkey in the Peanuts

Patrick had never seen a ship so close up before, let alone the belly of such a mastodon. *Jonah in the whale,* he thought. He could count the happy memories at his school desk on one hand, but the lessons in religious history would certainly be among them. When Mr. Baldwin had related the unbelievable adventures of those Bible figures, the otherwise noisy class had hung on every word. Patrick could still hear his teacher's voice resonating in the classroom.

"Is anyone here?" Patrick called out. He was startled by the sound of his own voice, which rolled through the ship's hold and echoed back to him.

Mr. Hook had directed him to the gangway of the *Caesar.* "You'll see what you have to do with the nuts below," he had snarled. "I'll come later to check on how you're doing. Now get going!"

Patrick had crossed the gangplank and steel steps. Luckily he'd been able to make his way deep down into the bowels of the deserted ship. He had reached the cargo hold; that was certain. It smelled like rancid butter. The first rays of sun were white as snow and streamed obliquely in through three high portholes. Slowly his eyes grew used to the contrast of light and darkness. *There's no shortage of peanuts,* he thought when he saw the remnants of the cargo on the floor. The layer of nuts wasn't any thicker than a centimeter or two, but this iron whale of a ship was probably as long as a soccer field.

"Is anyone here?" he called more carefully this time. He thought he heard a distant shout rise above his echoes.

"Here in front!" he seemed to have heard. A tiny voice was coming from the left. Patrick stepped cautiously onto the ledge that ran in a bow along the side of the hold and walked toward the nose of the boat.

He discovered that the voice was coming from the very front of the hold. It belonged to a gaunt little fellow who looked at Patrick with suspicion. He was lying on a heap of burlap sacks piled on top of a long crate. Apparently the forecastle served as a storage area for bags and chests and as a place to sleep, too.

"Do *you* sleep here?" Patrick asked in surprise.

"You noticed," the boy replied. "It's still a lucky break, this ship. At least it's dry." He patted down his reddish hair and rubbed the sleep from his eyes, yawning.

He doesn't look well, Patrick thought when he saw the bags under his eyes.

"I'm Seamus," the boy said as he threw a heavy sack off his legs. He jumped up.

Patrick was confused. Because of the boy's small stature, Patrick had taken Seamus to be thirteen or fourteen. But now that Patrick had a better look and could see the sunken cheeks, Seamus seemed much older.

"Seamus," the boy repeated. "Welcome."

"Oh . . . I'm Patrick . . . Condon . . . Uh, I was sent here by Fatso—I mean, Mr. Hook. You know him, don't you?"

"Better than you think!"

Patrick noticed the bitterness in Seamus's voice. "Are any other . . . uh, men coming to work here?" he inquired. "Dockworkers, I mean."

Seamus sighed. "Hook prefers to keep the boys separated from the men."

"Maybe it's better that way," Patrick said.

"It depends on how you look at it. Yes, it's better for *him!*" Seamus rolled his eyes and shrugged his shoulders in disdain. "So you've come to pick up peanuts, Patrick. Fatso likes it when boys bend forward and scrape their knees for him."

Patrick had no idea what Seamus meant, but he fervently agreed with the boy that Archibald Hook was a real bastard.

"You can begin in the meantime," Seamus said. "Fill the sacks. Here they are." He pointed to a pile of burlap bags.

"What about you?"

"I'm going to pee over the railing and get myself a hunk of bread. I'll only be gone ten minutes. It would be better for you to have a brush or shovel handy when Fatso makes his rounds—otherwise he'll put *you* in the sack," Seamus warned, and he snickered.

Patrick wasn't especially clumsy, but filling that first sack turned out to be more difficult than he expected. *Luckily no one is around to see me botch this,* he thought. He held his heavy spade in one hand, and with the other hand he opened the mouth of the shapeless bag and shoveled peanuts in. Just as many nuts landed outside the bag as inside.

Seamus returned fifteen minutes later. He laughed himself silly when he saw that Patrick had scarcely begun to fill his second bag. "You won't even be halfway through by next year, Patrick!" he chuckled. "Look, this is the way you have to do it." From a corner in his improvised sleeping quarters he pulled out an iron stand, a sort of giant hat rack, and moved it to their work area. He hung two sacks upon it, then effortlessly aimed his first shovelful of peanuts into an open sack. Patrick spit into his hands and followed Seamus's example. A glance from one was taken as a challenge by the other, and each filled a bag in no time.

They spent hours working in one area that morning. It was like a contest, and Patrick could hold his own. He seemed to be stronger, but Seamus was handier. Seamus

needed to take a drink of water every now and then—
he had some trouble with his lungs, and the dust in the
boat did him no good. But he was obviously enjoying
the company of his new colleague. And despite the
heavy work, Patrick was in high spirits as a brand-new
dockworker. When Seamus stopped to catch his breath,
Patrick amused him with his silly antics, swinging from
one spanning to another near the top of the loading
area. By midday they had filled about a hundred large
sacks that were one and one-half meters in length and
had grouped them neatly together. Soon those sacks
would be hoisted up through a hatch.

"It's nice work," Seamus said, pointing to the bags,
"because we can eat in between loadings."

"Isn't there a lunch break?" Patrick asked, wiping the
dust from his eyelashes.

"Not for you, Condon!" a deep voice crackled right
behind him.

Patrick turned around and looked directly at Archibald Hook's fat stomach. The sweet aroma of peanuts
was overpowered by the stench of beer and sweat. Mr.
Hook thrust his belly forward and threw him a nasty
punch. Patrick flew two meters back and tumbled
against the wall of the hold.

"*You* come with me!" Mr. Hook beckoned to Seamus as he pointed to the sleeping quarters. During this whole time the boy had been cowering like a beaten dog. Slavishly he followed Mr. Hook's command.

"And you, Condon," the big man said, slurring his words, "go to the crane operator on the wharf and say that in a half hour we'll bring this freight up."

Patrick scurried away as fast as he could. The giant called after him, "And bring me a big bottle of cold beer from the Skipper, that café not far from here."

Patrick hesitated. "But I have no money."

"Have them put it on my tab, damn it! Now get out of my sight!"

That slave driver Archibald Hook had an odd concept of "not far," for Patrick had walked for at least fifteen minutes. He found the Skipper to be more like a plush theater than a café. It was even darker inside than in the belly of the ship, and there were many strange women walking about, all heavily perfumed and scantily dressed. The customers weren't used to seeing boys his age on the premises, and they looked up in surprise when he entered. But the owner of the café knew Mr. Hook and didn't make trouble.

Patrick hurried back to the wharf, convinced that he'd be scolded for being late. Breathlessly he dove down the last stairwell to the forecastle. Suddenly a strange feeling overcame him.

Rising above his own panting were sounds from the half darkness, stifled, panic-stricken cries from Seamus and snorting growls from a furious Fatso. Chests and planks were crashing against the walls. Patrick crept closer and hid behind the filled bales. His heart was beating in his throat. Seamus was across from him; wild-eyed, he was waving a shovel defiantly at Mr. Hook. Patrick had never seen a face so filled with hate and despair. Mr. Hook was standing with his back against the sacks. Sweat ran in streams among the folds of his neck.

"You'll be sorry for this, you little shit!" he roared, taking a step forward.

It was then that Patrick noticed the unbelievably huge, white, hairy backside of the man. At the same time he realized that the rags piled on top of the sacks were Mr. Hook's trousers.

I don't want to lose my job, not on the first day. Patrick's thoughts were racing. *My father will kill me if I come to blows with that bum. Where would we find other work?* His heart was beating like a sledgehammer. For a moment he exchanged glances with Seamus. The boy straightened his shoulders with newfound courage and tightened his grip on the shovel.

"Get back, you pig!" Seamus shouted. "I have nothing more to lose!" He swung the shovel, grazing the buttons on the man's shirt.

Carefully Patrick lifted his head above the sacks and gestured to Seamus to calm down. Then he raised his thumbs high and scampered to the stairs.

"Okay, all the hatches can be opened!" Patrick called to the crane operator and the handful of dockhands who had been brought to help. Immediately the operator led the way and pulled open one of the panels.

Never had there been a more beautiful spectacle in any Waterford theater than the farce that had played out in the hold of the *Caesar* that day. The grand finale had been the monster's escape. Mr. Hook had run across the cobblestones of the wharf with a jute sack wrapped around his middle.

"And where are his trousers?" asked Seamus, when he heard about what had happened.

"I've no idea," Patrick answered, winking.

When they were through hoisting up the last of the bales from the ship, only an enormous wad of cloth remained on the floor. For a long time afterward those trousers were kept behind the bar of a local pub. Every once in a while they were brought out and displayed like a trophy.

TWO YEARS LATER
June 1913
South Ireland

Goodbye, Waterford?

Patrick looked across the rusty-brown backs of four oxen. The midday sun shone on their gleaming withers. He whistled as he passed his stick over their backs to chase away the flies, which swarmed the cattle market of Ballybricken on warm days. He liked this job. Whenever he and his brothers couldn't find work at the harbor in the mornings, they headed home right away. They could always charm a few cattle dealers into letting them tend their stock while negotiating a sale or clinching a deal in the nearby cafés. And if the brothers couldn't find work at the market, they could always offer a hand at O'Sullivan's, the brewery in the center of the city. But the job of dockworker paid the best. Sometimes they could also do business in lost goods or cargo remnants, but that was backbreaking labor, even for a tough, sturdy fellow like Patrick.

"In a year or two or three, you'll be stronger and faster than all of us," the dockhands said generously. "But you'll have to grow a head taller." The men at the wharf had taken a liking to him, but when jobs were scarce, it was every man for himself.

Patrick couldn't wait another two years. He had very quickly settled down in the harbor and felt good among those strapping men. Besides, anything was better than school. But before long, his old flame came knocking again—he wanted to become a soldier, and he let everyone know it. He could talk forever about the drummer boys and buglers who had accompanied the Duke of Marlborough to the European battlefields in days gone by; or about the powder monkeys, who had had to supply the cannons for Lord Nelson's fleet in the Battle of Trafalgar; or about the fourteen-year-old boys who served in Queen Elizabeth's Royal Navy. He knew it all. Whenever navy boats were moored in the area, you couldn't tear him away. Not long ago he went missing for two days, until his father dragged him from a frigate and kicked him back to Ballybricken.

One thing was drummed into his ear during that adventure: "You must be sixteen to join the army." *If my father lets me lie about my age to get work, then I can add a few years for the army, too,* Patrick mused. He was hatching a plan.

I should have left a note, certainly for my mother, Patrick thought. But writing was not his strongest suit. He kept a brisk pace and pursued his tall skipping shadow in a westward direction. It would soon become completely light. His eyes followed the winding dirt road to where the towers of Fiddown loomed above the rising mist in the distance. The grass along the shoulders gradually gained more color from the stark-white chervil and the bright-red poppies. On the slopes, the yellow tracts of coleseed now pierced through the haze. The birds in the shrubs twittered to one another. Patrick breathed deeply, taking in the smells of the herbs that grew here.

He could tell by the milky-white sunlight penetrating through the mist that it was going to be a glorious day.

Patrick was beginning to relax. He had succeeded in slipping away from home without having been seen. He couldn't go back now. A vague mix of relief and remorse crept over him. He had cut the cord, but he had disappeared like a thief in the night, without saying goodbye. He didn't want to hurt his mother and two sisters, although he strongly suspected that they had known he was up to something. *If all goes well, I'll write them a letter, even if it's just a short one,* he thought to comfort himself.

"Louder!" shouted the man with a red mustache.

"Sorry, *sir!*" said Patrick, a bit more forcefully now. Quickly he removed his hat and put it under his arm.

"Don't say sorry!" barked the man, red-faced. "Name?"

Patrick felt his shoes pinching his aching feet. The thirty-mile trek to Clonmel had not agreed with him. He was terribly tired and flustered, and now this little tyrant was breaking his eardrums.

"John Condon, *sir!*"

"John? *John!* Is that your name?"

Patrick's heart skipped a beat. *This man can't possibly know my real name,* he was thinking.

"John, eh?" roared the little man, who was right in front of his face now.

Patrick felt the tips of their shoes touch. The man's breath was horrible. And what a strange, filthy brown uniform he was wearing! Patrick had heard about these new khaki outfits of the professional army, but he didn't think much of them.

"Hear that, Corporal? His name is John!" The awful face turned to the man at the writing table. "And surely Condon is his first name?" he snickered.

The corporal forced himself to appear amused. He shrugged his shoulders.

"Uh, my name is Condon, *sir.*" Patrick could barely finish his sentence.

"HOLD! YOUR! TONGUE!" roared the corporal with renewed energy. "Has ANYONE asked you?"

"No, sir." Patrick hardly dared to answer. It had been a long time since he'd had a crying fit, but he could feel one coming on now.

"And stop calling me *sir!*" The whiskered man put

one of his sleeves forward. "Three stripes and another two under them. That's sergeant major. And *sir*—that's for officers. Is that clear?"

"Yes, Sergeant Major," Patrick ventured to say. Ever since he'd been a toddler, he had known all the ranks, stars, and stripes by heart, even the complicated sleeve piping of the navy. And Patrick certainly was aware that this man was a noncommissioned officer. But how was *he* to know what to call him?

The corporal finally wrote down Patrick's name and address. Then came the most sensitive subject of all.

"Age?" barked the sergeant as he circled him.

Patrick pulled his shoulders up a bit more in order to appear heavier. He knew that this man, who had experience with recruits, was assessing him. The boy shut his eyes and hesitated a little. "Seventeen, Sergeant Major," he finally answered boldly.

For a moment it was quiet. Patrick had added on five years. Would they fall for it? His brother John was exactly five years older than he. Thus they could safely check the office of records in Waterford.

"Do you have a letter of recommendation with you, Condon?"

"I hadn't thought to get one, Sergeant Major," Patrick lied. He was trying to hide his relief over his previous lie. Everything was going to be all right!

"Come back tomorrow for the physical, Condon. If you pass it, I see no reason why you can't be placed on the recruit list for part-time soldiers. Okay, dismissed!" the sergeant major commanded. He turned to the corporal. "Next!"

As Patrick was heading for the door, the sergeant major called to him. "Oh, Condon, one more thing . . ."

Here it comes, thought Patrick. *He's on to me.*

The man removed his cap and pointed to his close-cropped head. "From now on, comb that lousy hair of yours. It's full of straw." He could barely suppress a smile.

Patrick breathed with relief, yet he was confused. *Idiot,* he reproached himself. That morning he had carefully brushed off his clothes after crawling out of the haystack, hadn't he? He reached up to touch his hair—he apparently had forgotten to tend to the straw up there. He smiled back, thanked the sergeant, and limped out the door. His eyes were filled with tears, which were as much from happiness as from the terrible blisters his worn-out shoes had given him.

A Soldier at Last

Patrick had never before been as far as the city of Clonmel. Once he and his mother had traveled to Dunmore East, a cozy little fishermen's harbor half a day's walk to the south. There they had visited his mother's sister, who was gravely ill. She lived in an earthen hut on the west bank of the St. George's Channel, near the Irish Sea. Aunt Ella . . . They weren't a moment too soon, for she died the next day.

And here he was, a full day's journey from Waterford,

all alone, on the border of County Tipperary. What would his family think? "One less mouth to feed," his father would growl, but also, "A wage earner gone, and a nuisance, too." Father probably wasn't very upset. His mother, on the other hand—she usually remained silent in family disputes, to keep the peace, but he knew she'd be concerned.

My worries are short-lived, in any case, Patrick thought. *In a few days I'll be a soldier at last. Even though I'll be part-time, it means that I'll get free food and clothes and who knows, maybe even a roof over my head, too. I'll have to look out for myself until then.*

He touched the small leather pouch that dangled on a string under his shirt. At home, he had had to hand over every last cent of his wages. Pocket money had been out of the question. But those little jobs that he occasionally had gotten at the harbor had supplied him with a nice stack of pennies. He had secretly put aside these extra earnings for two whole years.

Clonmel was a city that had everything, including cheap lodgings above the many cafés. Yet Patrick chose the known over the unknown. He went out beyond the city, where the police didn't ask questions, and fell into conversation with a slightly drunk farm hand named Roy, who was returning from the market. They quickly reached an agreement over the price of lodging. Patrick got a spacious bedroom with a breathtaking view of the glowing valley, high and dry in a secluded barn. *What a bed,* he thought when he nestled in the hay. At home they all lay snoring together in one room. The barn was barely a ten-minute walk from the army barracks, straight across the fields and pastures. "You can wash up in the river below," Roy told him cheerfully. "And one more thing: no smoking."

Patrick paid for three nights in advance, in case he failed the physical. To his great relief, the farm hand, according to their agreement, returned that evening with half a loaf of bread, some cheese, and a bottle of watery beer. What more could a young vagabond want?

The doctor, an army captain, found nothing wrong with Patrick's condition. On the contrary. Together with five other men—Patrick thought some were fairly old—he was thoroughly examined. The corporal from the previous day recorded all the personal information: height, weight, and hair and eye color. Patrick then received a shot in his left arm.

"A bit thin, perhaps, for a seventeen-year-old boy," declared the doctor, and he winked. "But certainly fit enough for the Militia Battalion."

Patrick was floating. Imagine—the Militia Battalion! How his family would look up to him! Every Irishman knew about these militias. During the past three centuries, every powerful landowner had his own private army, manned by local inhabitants who worked part-time there. Meanwhile, those battalions made up a part of the regular British troops in Ireland. And he, Patrick Condon, had been inducted. Men from his neighborhood would be green with jealousy when they found out. *The Militia Battalion!*

Patrick had trouble keeping up a tough appearance later that day. Three other recruits were going to the city to drink to their good outcome. Patrick didn't dare refuse when he was asked to join them. He was at least as excited as the other three put together, but he had no more experience with alcohol than most other twelve-year-old boys. After his fifth pint of dark stout, he'd had it, certainly when the others began standing in the doorway and calling out to anyone in a skirt—even calling out to old women of twenty-five years and up! Patrick staggered back to the farm. It took him a lot longer than ten minutes to reach the barn. Apparently the friendly farm hand had waited up for him, and he came knocking less than five minutes after Patrick's return, expecting to hear good news. And he had a well-filled hip flask with him.

Patrick himself couldn't say how the rest of the night turned out. The sun was already high in the sky when he awoke from his stupor. His breakfast went untouched that day.

What a Life!

Peas with bacon—mmm! Bacon with peas the next day. The day after that, the cook fell back to his first menu. Every once in a while, on days of great culinary inspiration, there was mutton stew on the table, and then Patrick felt as though he were back home again. But you never heard him complain about life in the barracks. Not at all!

He received intensive training for the first two weeks. The drill sergeant was the same bully who had recruited him, but Patrick was actually glad to be in the command of such a howler. The boy enjoyed marching in rhythm among a troop of other puppets, who whirled and twirled wherever and whenever the lion tamer wished. As long as he dutifully did as he was told, the drillmaster's yelling didn't seem so offensive. Patrick liked being part of such a well-oiled military machine. After a couple of days, stepping from the barracks toward the drilling field to the cadence of "left-right-one-two" even gave him a pleasant tingling sensation in his belly. He belonged here—he had waited for this for such a very long time. As the youngest in the corps he was certainly the least important, but marching among the rows of recruits gave Patrick a completely new feeling of power.

Two weeks of being a full-time soldier in training couldn't stretch out long enough for him. Patrick liked target practice the best. It was a little game of dexterity and precision: ready your weapon, take aim at the target, hold your breath, pull the trigger . . . and then feel the shock that jolted through your entire body. Even the smell of sulfur from the exploded cartridges gave him a buzz. They should have seen him here, those good-for-nothings in the streets of Ballybricken, who perhaps were now fighting over a pound of bruised apples or a young bird. He, Patrick Condon of Wheelbarrow Lane, alias John Condon, had a gun in his hand—a gun with real bullets! As a part-time soldier, he wouldn't often get a chance to use live ammunition. Therefore he enjoyed every shot he could fire under the approving eye of Sergeant Bully, who deeply appreciated Patrick's enthusiasm. The only activity that was somewhat unpleasant was bayonet practice. "But that's the last thing you'll ever have to use," the drillmaster assured them, and he kept the sessions brief.

It was truly a prince's life: playing soldier, three meals a day, free clothes—luckily not those modern, dirty khaki things—a bed, and a salary for all this, besides!

Patrick had chosen to live in the barracks during his training. Whoever lived nearby was allowed to sleep at home. He had talked to Roy about the possibility of returning to the farm after the two weeks, for he would then have to find a permanent roof over his head as well as a second part-time job.

The boy had just one worry: home. Sometimes the thought wakened him. It was high time he wrote to Waterford. Maybe everything would be all right when they heard that he was earning an honest living. But he wouldn't write just yet, for he was much too busy.

"Condon, eh?" asked the somewhat older man who was ladling the soup.

Patrick suddenly forgot to hold out his mess tin. He had a vague feeling that he'd met this man before, but with the white kitchen hat and spotless apron that blinded him in the midday June sun, the boy couldn't see his face very well. The fellow behind him poked him in the ribs.

"Uh, John, uh, Condon, that's right," he stammered in surprise. He was still getting used to his first name. "How did you know . . ."

"Hey!" a voice from the line interrupted impatiently. "Can't you choose between soup and soup?"

Patrick quickly put his tin forward.

"Tom," replied the server, and he nodded with a smile. He ladled deep into the kettle and treated Patrick to a full portion of soup with lots of pieces of oxtail. "Pay no attention to those farm boys behind you," he said quietly. "Ranting like that won't get them their meal a minute sooner." He leaned forward. Patrick judged the cook's mate to be at least forty-five.

"You know where to find me if you need anything," Tom added, and he winked.

"Hey!" The voice from the back was louder now.

"All right, all right!" Tom answered.

Patrick quickly moved along with his overflowing soup tin. He sat down at one of the unoccupied tables in the courtyard. How did he know this Tom? Was it at the harbor in Waterford? The cattle market in Ballybricken, perhaps? He was searching his memory in vain, trying to place the kitchen worker's face. For a few seconds he feared that the man was among the dissatisfied customers from one of those countless jobs he'd had in the harbor. But no, this man's friendliness had appeared genuine.

Patrick slurped the delicious soup. Eating outside in this weather was wonderful, better than being in that stuffy soldiers' mess in the barracks. He concentrated on fishing out the last pieces of meat.

"The King's Arms," a deep voice called.

Patrick's spoon fell into the soup. He saw the cooking hat right in front of him.

"The café right here in Clonmel . . ."

It began to dawn on Patrick. He had forgotten the name of the pub, but of course *that* was it: last week, the fifth Guinness, which they had toasted to their success—this man had paid for that round.

"Tom! Of course!" exclaimed Patrick, a little too enthusiastically now. He couldn't have remembered the man's name for a million pounds.

"Weren't you having fun then?"

"Just give me a good bowl of soup," answered Patrick, and he laughed. He had no desire to talk about his hangover. "Do you work here in the kitchen, Tom?"

The man removed his hat. "Every now and then. It's a nice job, I tell you. Lots of variety. You get that after working here almost thirty years." He extended his hand. "Thomas Carthy, born and bred here in Clonmel."

"John Condon," said Patrick.

"Call me Tom or Tommy. Where are you from, John?"

"Waterford."

"Port Láirge!"

"Right. Do you know the area?" Patrick asked. To his surprise, he felt immediately at ease with this man. Was it Tom's gaze, so direct but so friendly, too? Was it his soothing voice?

"The pig market. I was there once or twice with my uncle, when I was a young chap."

"Ballybricken?" asked Patrick, wide-eyed.

"Yes! That's what it's called, now that you mention it."

"That's where I'm from!" said Patrick, but he quickly caught himself. "You don't know anyone there by chance, do you?"

"Have you something to hide, John Condon?" Tom teased.

"Of course not. Why?" Patrick was completely unsettled. "Why should I?" he added, trying to recover from his outburst.

"A bright little guy you are . . . for your age."

"Carthy! Come here!" A thickly whiskered man with a cooking hat that was clearly taller than Tom's shouted over the table in their direction.

"That's the chief-cook-sergeant. Keep your chin up, John Condon!" Tom placed his white kitchen cap at an angle on his head and hurried back to the soup line.

TWO WEEKS LATER

June 20, 1913
CLONMEL, SOUTH IRELAND

Half Soldier

The heavy barrack door closed behind Patrick with a thud.

"See you soon, John!"

"See you later!"

The men's chattering to one another as they departed was turning into an unintelligible buzz.

"Get home safely!" a voice called cheerfully in the distance.

Wherever that *may be,* Patrick thought wistfully, even though the call hadn't been meant for him.

The gigantic bolt slid into the lock. The wooden bar moved into place with a dry cracking sound. The entrance to the army depot was closed for the night, sealed like a city gate in the Middle Ages—no one allowed in, no one allowed out.

"So, here you are, John," he said out loud to himself. "It's up to you now. If I can be you in the army, let's see if I can be you outside the army, too." He turned around and looked at the high wall of the barracks with deep respect. His training was over. *Part-time soldier, without a roof over my head,* he thought. *Half soldier and half good-for-nothing.* Seventeen years old to the outside world, much younger in his thoughts and in his heart.

As Patrick strolled toward the center of the city, he wondered how he was going to fill his life and his wallet in the coming months. As soon as he turned eighteen, so to speak, he wanted to try his luck as a professional soldier. In the meantime, he had to be careful not to fall out of his role as a seventeen-year-old. His very first concerns now were to find a second job and decent shelter.

He had not left the military domain in two weeks.

The barracks and grounds, the woods and stores, had become his new little world. The iron discipline and the harassing by the veteran soldiers had been tough to take. But he had been swept up by the genuine team spirit and unshakable enthusiasm of the recruits.

When Patrick saw the lights appear in the windows of the cafés, he realized that evening was fast approaching. He needed a place to sleep before dark. He hesitated. Should he go see Thomas Carthy, who perhaps could advise him? Or should he just rent a room in the city? Or simply return to that old, trusty barn, as he had planned? As he stared at the tips of his shoes, he noticed that shamrocks were blooming between the jagged cobblestones. He bent down and picked one. "A four-leaf clover," he called in surprise. *Summer begins tomorrow,* he realized. *A day to do something nice, a day to begin something new.*

He turned around. Fifteen minutes later, he lay stretched out in the straw. He had returned to the barn. No one would bother him there.

"Hey, soldier boy!" The voice sounded as if it were reverberating in the belly of a freighter.

Patrick rubbed the sleep from his eyes. *I didn't even take off my clothes or shoes,* he thought. *I must have fallen asleep right away.*

"It's afternoon, John," said the voice, which was nearby now. "The sun is already high in the sky. It's a shame to be sleeping in like this."

Startled, Patrick propped himself up on his elbows. A cone of glaring white light was coming straight through the open door and shining on his lower legs. He could see a silhouette in front of the door through his fluttering eyelashes.

"How about a hearty breakfast?"

"Roy, it's you!"

The farm hand threw a linen sack of provisions onto the straw next to the boy. "And here's a jug of fresh milk." He reached into a bin that stood outside the door.

"Thanks, Roy. This is fantastic. You haven't forgotten me," exclaimed Patrick, and lit into the food immediately. He was famished.

"Congratulations, little soldier! You withstood the test, I hear."

Patrick could only bring forth a few *mmms* and nod with enthusiasm as he chewed and chewed. He realized that Roy must have contacts in the city or in the barracks. Patrick washed down the hunks of bread with a slug of lukewarm milk, then decided to ask his question straightaway. "Would you have a job for me?"

Roy didn't seem a bit surprised. "Who knows," he answered. "But how's this going to work?" He rubbed his thumb over his pointing finger. "Cash down."

"All right, Roy. I'll pay you. Tomorrow, after my first real day of service, I'll get my first wages. A full two weeks' wages, you understand!"

"Not bad. I'm counting on you, John Condon."

How on earth does he know my last name? I never told him, thought Patrick.

"Can you do some farming?"

"For the time being, yes."

"These are busy days here. Crops to be tended, and soon the harvest. And then the animals. All help would be welcome, I think."

"Fine. When do I begin?" Patrick asked, a little too eagerly.

"Just a minute. I'll have to ask Mr. McGuinness first. Can you drive a team of horses?"

"As well as the best of them," Patrick lied. "And I'm good with cows, too. I worked at the cattle market in Waterford, you see. Ballybricken."

"Ten percent for me," said Roy, very businesslike. "And that's not a bad deal. Let me work it out with the farmer. I know what you should charge; you don't." He winked and clapped Patrick on the shoulder.

❧

The first workday in the barracks was like a dream. And it became more obvious with each task that this dream was real. Clonmel's reserve corps had recognized Patrick as a soldier—a part-time soldier, to be sure, not yet in the regular British Army. But still, he was a member of the military.

First they proceeded to the kitchen. Patrick and the five other recruits received their mess kits. The next stop was the tailor, who had worked very hard during the past two weeks, making a gray-blue two-piece uniform for each man. Patrick couldn't tear his eyes away. He thought it was wonderful, especially with the shoulders that displayed the insignia CLONMEL—COUNTY WATERFORD. A gold harp, the symbol of Ireland, gleamed on each lapel.

"These are your summer uniforms," the tailor explained. "There's still time enough to make the winter version."

The last stop was the arsenal. The gunsmith was a tall, wiry fellow around fifty years old who smelled like lubricating oil. On the workbench behind him was a revolver that had been completely disassembled. "Don't touch it," he warned when he saw Patrick's admiring gaze.

Patrick wanted to ask if it was a Belgian FN, but he thought that would be a bit inappropriate on his first day.

"Get this into your head," said the gunsmith in a clear but friendly way. "You may never come to this locale alone or without permission." Slowly and carefully he allowed his gaze to pass along the six faces. "Anyway, it's always locked up tight, even when I'm here."

The recruits had already noticed the number of locks on the iron-fitted door and the grating in front of it.

"And your rifles are behind the screen."

Patrick watched in suspense as the man pulled on an iron roll-down shutter from above and revealed about thirty rifles. They were hanging neatly from a rack, and all were double locked with a steel bar and a chain.

"Remember your number, and always set your weapon back in the same space." The chain jingled furiously as the gunsmith pulled it through the many rings, allowing it to fall in a heap next to his feet.

The recruits were each handed a rifle, one by one. Even though Patrick and his comrades had drilled with such a weapon dozens of times, this was completely new, for each of them now had his own rifle, his own personal weapon. Patrick was a real soldier now—or rather, a half soldier.

Half Farmer

Patrick had guard duty at the arsenal two, sometimes three, days a week, and he had the night watch every now and then. It wasn't really an exciting occupation, except for the time a stag got his antlers caught in the fence. It had been pitch-dark. The animal had created such a ruckus that Patrick and his mate were scared to death. They thought it was a burglar and even fired a warning shot. That shot elicited considerable moaning from the commander, and the soldiers joked about the incident for weeks. But Patrick loved this man's world, even though he had hoped for more action.

❦

There was plenty of action on the farm during that summer of 1913. Roy arranged a sweet little deal between Patrick and Mr. McGuinness. Of course, he remembered to take his own cut, too. Patrick received room and board on the large farmstead. He set up a modest room next to Roy's, above the horse stalls. It was nice and warm at night and cozy, too, with the sounds of the animals below. However, it was a room that had quite a smell.

Paul McGuinness was an energetic, hard-working young man. Together with his wife, Sinead, they had taken over the farm from her uncle.

"Whoever is willing to roll up his sleeves is welcome, certainly in the summer," he said when Patrick had been introduced to him. "How old are you, John?"

"Seventeen, sir."

"Just call me Paul." The farmer was a down-to-earth fellow. Patrick could see that Roy was crazy about him.

"What a coincidence. My youngest brother, Brian, is also seventeen. He's in Dungarvan, down on the coast. That's where we're from."

"Oh, really?" said Patrick, somewhat carelessly.

"In what year were you born, John?"

"Nine . . ." Patrick faltered and felt the blood rush to his face. *Nineteen-oh-one,* he'd almost blurted out. He could tell that Paul had noticed his slip. "One . . . one of my brothers is named Brian, too," he lied as he managed a sick laugh.

"Another coincidence," said Paul, and he chuckled.

Paul McGuinness was very flexible. Patrick gave him his work schedule at the barracks and was allowed to help out on the farm as often as he wanted. He quickly felt at home there. *I'm more at ease here than I was on Wheelbarrow Lane,* he thought. He was a bit uneasy with this realization.

Trapped!

Plowing, harrowing, sowing, tending the animals. It seemed like a crash course in farming. Patrick helped out as much as he could and earned a substantial salary for his efforts. Usually he worked alongside Paul and Roy, who were diligent drudges but always good-humored. The two of them laughed through the oppressive July and August heat that hung over South Ireland. Patrick rose to the challenge and plodded along, though it took effort to keep up with them.

Patrick appeared to have a remarkable way with animals. He could effortlessly harness the two horses in the morning and unhitch them in the evening. Paul quickly noticed this and sometimes let him drive the team, allowing him to take the fully loaded wagon from the field to the farm and sometimes even to nearby customers in Clonmel. Whenever Patrick had a free evening, he helped milk the cows or feed the pigs without being asked. Paul McGuinness and his young wife were delighted with him. Even though they hadn't expressed it in so many words, that was what Roy had told him.

Patrick Condon had found his niche on the farm in no time at all, though occasionally he yearned for freedom, for the luxury of doing absolutely nothing. Sometimes he even considered returning to Port Láirge, to the guttersnipes of Waterford, and to the little house at number two Wheelbarrow Lane. His thoughts often dwelled on his mother. *What would she be doing now? What would she be thinking?* he wondered.

The hardest thing for Patrick was being with men and having to listen to their racy jokes and other crude talk, especially when girls were around. The language itself didn't bother him; in fact, he thought all that macho talk was cool. But he didn't always understand their slang when women were discussed. He hadn't learned anything from his sisters in that regard, especially at that low level. At the Waterford harbor, he had often had the feeling that the dockworkers were laughing twice: first at their own coarse jokes or dirty remarks, and then at him. He knew that his army comrades had chuckled more than once at his expense, but he had simply shrugged it off and tried to come back with a clever remark of his own.

During that summer on the farm, it struck Patrick that Moira, Sinead McGuinness's giggling maid, followed him around a lot. At first he hadn't noticed. But then he began to pay attention. Whenever Moira had a free moment or if Mrs. McGuinness was out for a bit, she slipped away and flitted around him—in the fields, in the barn, among the cows. She was amazingly spry, for once she even jumped up onto a moving manure cart and sat down next to him on the coach box. Moira was a cheerful girl, to be sure. But why did she always have to lean on him when she wanted to tell him something?

She was sixteen, "and that's the honest truth," Roy had said with a knowing wink as he outlined the girl's buxom figure with his hands.

One day, Moira was standing right behind Patrick just when he wanted to climb the ladder to the hayloft. Suddenly she threw her arms around his waist and held him tightly as she pushed her hips against his backside. He let out a yelp, for he was scared to death. Roy came at once to see what the commotion was about. Moira rushed out the door like a frightened chicken.

But she was back again the next afternoon. Patrick was dozing in bed. They had all just tucked into some barley gruel, which they had shared from a single large bowl on the kitchen table. There was still some work to be done in the stalls, but first Patrick went up to his loft for a while. The days were long, and the early-evening sun streamed in through the three windows, right into his face. He could perceive the sharp rays even with his eyes closed. Suddenly a black curtain blotted out the orange glimmer. A soft panting at the foot of his bed prompted him to bolt up immediately. In the background light, the sharp silhouette of Moira's upper body was visible through her thin white blouse. Bewildered, he tried to call out but could manage only a pitiful little squeak.

"Shh," Moira said in a hushed tone. She put a finger over her mouth and sat down on the bed next to him. Patrick sat on his blanket like an infatuated young child, paralyzed yet staring with rapt attention. He noticed that only the two bottom buttons of her blouse were fastened. The rest—oh God, what was he to do? How pretty she was! But he couldn't do this, not now, not yet . . .

"There, there," she said. Patrick could feel her hot breath in his right ear.

"Moira," he called now, louder than he wanted.

She grabbed him by the shoulders, pushed him down on the bed, and positioned herself above him. "Come on, John," she groaned.

"John! John!" called a voice beneath the loft.

"Roy! Roy? Is that you?"

"Yes, who did you think?" Roy answered, and he laughed. "Are you coming down or what?"

Patrick could hear Roy's footsteps on the bottom rungs of the ladder. "I'm coming, Roy!" He reached the steps with a giant leap. Before he backed down the ladder, he caught Moira's angry gaze and read an unmistakable *Damn!* on her lips.

The Letter

A yellowish light was flickering in the little room above the horse stall. It came from an oil lamp, which hung on a string that had been fastened to one of the roof ridges. Patrick was sitting on a milk stool, hunched over a small plank that rested on his knees. He lay his pen on the bed and read through the letter one last time.

CLONMEL, 3 SEPTEMBER 1913

Dear Father, Mother, Kate, Peter, Margaret,
and John,

This letter will certainly come as a
surprise. As you can see, I'm alive and well.
And I have good news. Maybe it will sound
unbelievable, but I've been a part-time
soldier for about two months now. What do you
think of that? I tried my luck at the local
county militia here in Clonmel. I had to bluff
my way through, because they won't take boys
my age (just like at the harbor). But I had
nothing to lose. If the militia had turned me
down, I'd have come back to Port Láirge and
spent my life at the docks or at the brewery.

Oh, and I'm called John here, when you
write back to me.

Mother, I'm sorry if I hurt you. You know
me better that anyone—you know that I've
always wanted to be a solider. And you know
that I'll be all right. I should have told you
goodbye, but I was afraid that you'd all laugh
at me for trying to join the militia.

Father, I'm truly sorry. I hope I can explain it to you again someday. But remember, I'm earning more here than I did in Waterford. When I have time off, I work on a farm for people who are very good to me.

Father and Mother, if it's all right with you, I'll do my best to come home soon. By Christmas at the latest, if the commander lets me. What do you think? Anyhow, don't worry about me. I have lots to eat and good clothes. And if I come, I will bring along my savings, which is more money than I could have ever earned at home.

Tell everyone I said hello, including Mollie and the baby. And the reverend and Mr. Baldwin, who will be reading this to you. Ask him to write back so that I'll know about coming for Christmas. I'll wait for your answer.

Your son,
Patrick

P.S. Again, please address your letter to JOHN Condon.

Patrick had swiped the sheets of paper from the guardroom of the barracks. At the newspaper store, he had bought a postage stamp and two envelopes, one extra in case he made a mess of the first one. For weeks he had kept the writing paper under his pillow; his thoughts had needed time to ripen.

Patrick wasn't fluent with a pen. He had chosen his words very carefully, but he had particularly grave misgivings over the part about his false name. He was especially afraid that his parents would send someone to bring him home for good or even write a letter to the army commander.

Patrick held his breath as he slipped the letter into the post office mailbox. And for the first time since that five-pint drinking binge, he went to the King's Arms, to wash away his emotions.

Then he began to wait impatiently for a reply.

The Tension Grows—in Europe, Too

Days turned into weeks, and weeks into a month. Still there was no answer.

"No, boy, no mail for you today," the corporal in the guardroom would say with a sigh when Patrick made his daily visit. He dropped by to check even when he was off duty.

"A girl in Port Láirge, eh?" the corporal had called to him a couple of times with an amused wink. "Maybe you should go visit her!"

It's not a girl. It's my mother, Patrick would think.

October had arrived. It looked as though life had quieted down on the McGuinness farm. The weather was raw and chilly. Gradually all the chores were being done indoors. The animals were spending more and more time in their stalls, and most of the work went toward feeding and caring for them. Patrick was still welcome; he kept his room above the horses and felt at home there, but he really wasn't needed any longer. He helped out with the upkeep of the machinery and buildings every so often. He now took his meals in the barracks as frequently as he could, even though Paul and Mrs. McGuinness never charged him a cent for food.

In any case, Patrick greatly enjoyed army life. All part-time soldiers who were available were given the chance to rack up more service hours than usual. "It all has to do with the Home Rule Bill," the boy would hear. It was obvious that this new law was often discussed among his colleagues, but not when their superiors were around. Ever since last year, when the London Parliament had promised to give Ireland more independence, tensions had been surfacing all over the country. Public speeches were delivered in halls and squares. Supporters of an Irish Catholic republic were being confronted by Protestants who preferred to stay under British rule, especially in the north. Patrick was indifferent to politics, but the situation was favorable to him and his companions because it meant more work. Vigilance was markedly stepped up, even in the south. Guard duty took on a certain grimness; Patrick felt that it wasn't a game anymore.

At the same time, politicians and generals all over Europe were preparing for something much bigger. They were anxiously watching Germany as it became a military giant, ready to conquer the entire continent. Could war be avoided for much longer?

"There's something in the air," the oldest soldiers whispered, and Patrick understood that they were talking about more than just this Home Rule on which so many Irish had pinned their hopes.

"The old continent is stirring up a hornet's nest again," Thomas Carthy claimed when the boy went to see him. Patrick was visiting his pal more and more often now. Tom lived with his wife, Mary, in a stone cottage at 34 River Street. They had no children, even though Tom was forty-five years old.

"What?"

"The Kaiser," Tom began gravely. He moved his feet a little closer to the red-hot brazier of the peat stove. "I don't know anything about politics," he continued, "but it looks like the Germans need more room. Factories are springing up out of the ground like toadstools. They're rich but they want more land."

"Who says?" Patrick asked.

"Sooner or later those Fritzes will break loose, I tell you." Without commenting further, Tom waved a newspaper that had been lying behind him on an easy chair.

Patrick shrugged. He had never held a newspaper before in his life.

"Lebensraum," Tom tried to pronounce in his best German. "The papers say that they want more living space."

"But Germany is a huge, huge place," Patrick suggested earnestly.

"Even though they're very rich, they're limping behind other countries," Tom explained like a seasoned schoolteacher. "If you calculate how spread out the French domain is, with all its colonies, and then there's the British Empire—"

"Where the sun never sets," Patrick solemnly chimed in.

"So big that those English even have to grab up Ireland," grumbled Tom's wife, who seldom spoke.

"No politics, woman!" Tom curtly reprimanded her.

And what are we *talking about, then?* Patrick wondered as he winked at Mrs. Carthy. Not wanting to add fuel to the fire, however, he kept that thought to himself. "Will we be called up more often now? Because of the Germans?" he asked.

"Of course. There's still the Home Rule, but those Fritzes, they play a part, too."

"Will there be a war?"

"Oh, it probably won't come to that. Let's hope."

"Well, I'd like to teach that Kaiser a lesson." Patrick raised his fist up into the air.

Tom and Mrs. Carthy burst out laughing.

TWO WEEKS LATER
October 1913
CLONMEL, SOUTH IRELAND

A Rude Awakening

"I can't pass up this chance!" Patrick's eyes sparkled as he looked at Thomas Carthy.

"You've got to be at least eighteen," exclaimed his friend, and he winked. That gesture removed all doubt; Tom was on to him.

"Eighteen? That can be arranged, Tom," Patrick answered, laughing boldly. "My God! The Special Reserve! Not the real army, but almost!"

"You have a fair chance. There's a big demand for soldiers. They'll be recruiting in Waterford. You'll be able to go home again."

"Home, yes . . ." Patrick grew quiet all of a sudden. "They never did get in touch with me after I sent my letter."

Patrick didn't want to burn any bridges as he rushed away from Clonmel. He had just gotten settled in there.

"Whatever happens, you needn't feel ashamed to return," Tom said as they discussed the possibilities. "If your plans fall through, just come back to work here after your furlough. And if you're accepted into the Special Reserve, there's still a good chance you'll be stationed here in Clonmel. Thus we hold with the hare and run with the hounds."

Tom knew what to do and quickly arranged everything for Patrick. Because the boy had put in extra service hours, he had earned a week's leave. It was enough time to travel home and try his luck at recruitment into the Special Reserve. And he had time to hurry back to the army depot in Clonmel if need be. He wrote a letter of resignation in which he thanked everyone for the chances he'd been given. He was careful to stress the fact that he wasn't leaving the army; on the contrary, he wanted to advance in the military. Tom kept the letter and promised to make sure that the colonel would receive it if Patrick didn't return on the appointed day. If the boy failed to make the Special Reserve, he would simply come back after his week's leave.

"You're more than a second father to me," he whispered a bit shyly to Tom. "You're a true friend."

Immediately after his last evening on duty, Patrick went as planned to the Carthys at 34 River Street. He knocked twice. Then he knocked again. Tom opened the front door.

"Ah, finally," Patrick said curtly. The heat from the peat stove blasted him in the face.

"Did everything go all right?" Tom asked.

The boy nodded. "Is Mrs. Carthy here?"

"She's sleeping."

"Does she know anything?"

Tom shrugged. "What she doesn't know won't hurt her. Come, let's quickly run through the plans again."

"Okay, but first this." Patrick reached into his pocket

and pulled out an envelope. "For the McGuinnesses. Will you give it to them? They've done everything for me."

Tom took the letter hesitantly.

"And this is for Roy." Patrick gave Tom a bank note. "I owe him money. This should be enough. Tell him that I . . ." He felt a lump rising in his throat.

"You can count on me," said Tom.

"He wouldn't be able to read a letter anyway," said Patrick hoarsely.

Fifteen minutes later, a shadowy figure walked along the house façades and out of the city of Clonmel. Patrick was somewhat conflicted. He could still feel his friend heartily embracing him when they'd said goodbye to each other, almost like a father would to a son.

He quickened his pace. He figured that he had at least a twelve-hour walk ahead of him. He needed to stop during the journey in order to grab a quick bite. He would be smarter this time, staying on the main roads and hitching as many rides off horse cars as possible. After all, Waterford was a long way, even for a trained soldier.

Just four short months ago, Patrick had traveled

this same route in the opposite direction, with wild ideas and a head full of questions. Although different thoughts haunted him tonight, at least as many questions were running through his mind. How would the people of Waterford react to his visit? His friends, the street tramps, the stray dogs, but especially those at home . . .

A strong wind began to blow, dry and ice cold. *My leather cap,* he thought, shrugging his shoulders. He reached into his knapsack and took out a warm wool-lined hat. He pulled the earflaps down against the raised collar of his jacket. He put his everyday hat into his duffel bag and groped farther down to make sure his military cap wasn't getting wrinkled. *As long as the weather stays dry, I'll be content,* he thought. With a bowed head he walked briskly on toward home, his real home.

It was in the afternoon of the next day that Patrick looked across the wide, watery expanse of the Three Sisters and recognized the towers of Port Láirge in the distance. They had never looked so beautiful. The biting wind was blowing over the rivers and causing his lips to feel chapped. In spite of the discomfort, he stopped and stared, motionless, for many minutes. The harbor was surprisingly quiet on a Sunday; there were no trails of smoke or steam rising from the ships.

Patrick walked along the River Suir toward home. The clock tower of the Holy Trinity chimed once. The tower of Christ Church chimed immediately afterward, followed by the clocks of the smaller, more modest parish churches in the distance.

He turned away from the river and walked toward the center of the city. The streets were deserted. Residents were eating a meal or taking a nap to get ready for a rough workweek. Even though he felt warm, Patrick kept his coat buttoned all the way up. He was approaching his neighborhood now. His heart was beating in his throat.

"If that's not Patrick Condon, I'll eat my hat!" he heard someone call out far behind him. He turned around in surprise. Two familiar heads appeared from behind a fence about a hundred meters away.

"Rogers and O'Sullivan!" Patrick exclaimed unwittingly. *I couldn't stand them and here I am now, waving as if we were old friends,* he said to himself angrily.

"Damn, Condon, it's *really* you!" Rogers looked at him as if he were the Virgin Mary.

"Patrick!" cried O'Sullivan in an overly friendly manner. "We thought you'd disappeared from the face of the earth!"

"I've come straight from Clonmel. The whole way on foot," he said. His voice no doubt sounded deeper and more serious than before.

"You seem older, Patrick," exclaimed O'Sullivan, and he laughed. "Everyone thought you'd fallen into the water. *We* didn't believe it, of course." He nudged Patrick with a conspiring look.

"Why did you go to Clonmel?" Rogers wanted to know. "Wasn't Waterford good enough for you?"

Patrick gazed about and saw that the street was still deserted. Slowly he opened his overcoat, one button at a time. The two boys watched, puzzled. Then they saw the copper clasp of his broad coupling strap and the gold buttons down his middle glimmering in the afternoon light. He exposed the lapels of his collar and let the gilded Irish harps flicker in the weak autumn sun.

"Damn, Condon . . ." was all Rogers could manage to say.

O'Sullivan studied him from head to toe for a good ten seconds while no one said a word. Patrick hesitated a moment, then pulled his army cap from his duffel bag and set it on his head.

"Wow! *Wooow!*" the two boys cried in chorus.

Patrick couldn't let the pleasure end there. He decided to remove his overcoat. *I'll show them the shoulder insignias of Clonmel,* he thought.

A bit farther up, another five heads appeared over the fence.

Even though Patrick felt like quite the man amid the gazes of the street children, what he wanted most was to be completely alone when calling on his parents. He was constantly wondering how they would react. In the meantime, the number of children appearing from behind the fence was growing; there must have been twenty-five, and more kept coming. It was impossible to shake them off as he headed toward Wheelbarrow Lane. The news of his return had spread like wildfire, for more and more people were clamoring up to him. Everyone had questions to ask, and the children tried to touch him. Although Patrick attempted to remain friendly, he strode resolutely along as he passed the cattle market and turned onto his street.

"Patrick!" a shrill voice cried out all of a sudden.

The sound of his name chilled the marrow of his bones.

"Patrick!" The voice was louder and more anxious now.

He stiffened. The crowd moved aside for him.

"Mother . . ." His knapsack fell to the ground. A weeping woman with two screaming girls at her heels rushed up to him. They fell into each other's arms. Kate, his older sister, grasped his shoulders. Margaret, the younger, grabbed at his hips. With his eyes shut tight, he pressed his mother to his chest and listened to her sobs.

There he was after all those months, at number two Wheelbarrow Lane, home again at last.

"Stupid boy . . ." His mother shook her head. "Stupid boy," she repeated again and again. "How could you do such a thing to us?"

Patrick looked at the floor and dared only to steal an occasional shy, quick glance at his mother and sisters, who sat staring at him with red, uncomprehending eyes. His mother held his hand. She kept sniffing and wiping her eyes on her sleeve. Her face was happy and angry at the same time.

"Tell me now, where have you been?"

"Didn't you get my letter?" he asked in surprise.

"We did. Father took it to Mr. Baldwin because none of your brothers and sisters were in. We had no idea who in God's name could have written a letter. The only letter we'd ever received was when Aunt Ella lay dying."

"And did the teacher read my letter to you?" Patrick pressed on impatiently.

"He read it to your father. I wasn't there . . ." She broke into sobs.

Patrick felt helpless.

"When he heard the teacher say that the letter came from *you*, he tore it up immediately. He was furious—he scarcely wanted to know what was in it. He was going to kill you, he said! Your own father!"

Patrick cursed himself and wished that he had never returned. No, he wished that he had never run away from home in the first place.

"Where is Father now?" he suddenly called out in panic. "And John? And Peter?"

"Don't worry, they won't be coming home today,"

she assured him. "We wouldn't be sitting here if your father were around. Harsh words have been spoken about your possible visit."

"So you knew that I was coming after all?" he said, puzzled.

"Mr. Baldwin told me what was in the letter."

"But I didn't give the exact day of my arrival, did I?"

"No, but on Thursday evening we received your telegram."

"What telegram? I didn't send any—"

She held the message under his nose before he could finish.

```
Clonmel Post Office
Sender: John Condon, Militia
    Battalion of the City
Coming home Sunday./ STOP/
Everything's OK./ STOP/
Love/STOP
John, Tom, and Roy/STOP/
```

"The postman said that perhaps Tom and Roy were coming as well. Who are those two?" she asked.

Patrick stood as if he were nailed to the floor. At first

he was speechless. "Tom and Roy?" he suddenly sputtered. "I'll have to tell you about them. Tom and Roy!" He burst out laughing. "Those devilish sneaks! And you specifically sent Father away because you knew I was coming?"

"I persuaded your father to go with your brothers to visit his family in Tramore for the weekend. Mollie and the baby have gone to her parents for a few days."

"If only I'd known about it before! All this worry . . ." That Thomas Carthy had made the plans with Roy, who therefore knew everything! The thought of the inevitable confrontation with his father had kept him up for hours these past three nights. Those two in Clonmel had grown to know him well—so well that they'd conspired to help him!

"Were you afraid that Father would hurt me?" Patrick was serious now.

She nodded wordlessly.

For the first time in years, ever since he was a sweet, naive little fellow, Patrick stared long and hard into his mother's eyes. Her face revealed the difficulties he had caused her, how torn she was in choosing between him and his father. She waited silently while he searched for words.

A Recruit Again . . . and a Step Up

He was back home, even if it might be for only a short time. Just being called "Patrick" again felt wonderful. Sometimes his false name hindered him like an overly tight jacket. He talked and talked about his new life in Clonmel that Sunday afternoon through the entire evening. He noticed how quickly his mother perked up as he charmed her with his stories. He looked healthy and well dressed and he'd saved a pretty penny, besides. Perhaps the situation wasn't so bad after all. Father Condon would quickly come around, Patrick and his mother hoped, when he saw how much money his lost son had earned in such a short time. Patrick's dad had been out of work more often than ever during the past months, Patrick learned.

Father, Peter, and John were due home Monday afternoon. Over breakfast, Patrick arranged for his mother to speak privately with her husband as soon as he returned.

In the meantime, Patrick, using his alias, John Condon Jr., put on his civilian clothes and left for the city center of Waterford. He planned to inform the personnel at the army recruiting office how and when he could report for duty. Just before he entered the office, he ran into Sergeant Bixby, an old comrade of his father's.

"Ah, the little Condon!" he exclaimed. "Back home again, so I hear?"

Even though Sergeant Bixby didn't live far away, it was obvious that the news was spreading very quickly. Yet he made no mention of Patrick's military adventures in Clonmel. The boy sensed that the man knew more than most, although he might not know about his name change.

"So you want to be a recruit in the Special Reserve?"

Sergeant Bixby asked in a stern voice. "A bit early, eh, fellow?"

Patrick felt himself blush. Was his entire plan going to fall through?

"Or rather," the sergeant continued, "a bit late. They begin here at nine o'clock. Come back tomorrow . . . when you're eighteen."

He clapped him on the shoulder and walked on, leaving Patrick speechless.

There was little time for bickering in the Condon house later that day. Father and son barely exchanged words. The man had never been much of a gabber, but his silence hurt. Embarrassed, Patrick tried to start with "Sorry, Father," but was unable to say more. His father acted as if he hadn't heard him. The tension in the air could have been cut with a knife. His mother followed the two with eagle eyes but was more than satisfied that everyone in the house was at least keeping quiet.

After four o'clock, Father put his coat on "to see if there is work to be had in the city tomorrow." He disappeared for the rest of the day.

Patrick and his brother John grabbed the chance to talk freely about their adventures of the past months. Kate and Margaret hung on every word. Mother listened quietly as she folded the wash and prepared Patrick's favorite mutton stew.

OCTOBER 24, 1913
RECRUITING OFFICE, SPECIAL ARMY RESERVE
WATERFORD, SOUTH IRELAND

The Big Test

The preliminaries went faster than Patrick had feared. When asked his occupation, he wrote "bottler," a job that could be verified at Sullivan's Brewery. It was probably better not to put down "dockworker" because of that little incident with Fatso, even though it had been months ago. As for "cow watcher," that was something he'd been only sporadically at the cattle market. "Soldier" seemed totally dangerous, for imagine if they were to sift through his file in Clonmel. In the space marked "age," he had confidently marked "eighteen," a year older than what he had reported to the militia in June.

Obviously there was a great need for reservists. A tall boy who was turning eighteen in December got a second chance and a new application form with the comment that it would be better not to report an exact date of birth. Two old men and a slovenly fellow who reeked of gin a bit too early in the day were taken aside and whisked back to the street a few minutes later.

The names of the candidates were now called up one by one: "Adams, Condon, Connolly, Dempsey . . ." Patrick was the second to be examined by Major-Doctor Power. *Back to square one,* he thought as he stood there naked. *I've already played this little game.*

He was weighed and measured; his eyes were examined and he had to take some deep breaths. The doctor's only question concerned the scars on one leg—a souvenir from Clonmel, when Roy had been gathering hay and had torn Patrick's pants to shreds with his pitchfork.

The information for his medical file was notated in thick black pen strokes:

Stated age: 18 years

Occupation: bottler

Religion: Roman Catholic

Height: 5 feet 4 inches

Weight: 118 lbs.

Hair: brown

Eyes: brown

Vision: L & R, 6 on 6

Vaccinations: right 1, left 2 (infirmary)

Outstanding characteristics: 3 scars left thigh, outer side

"No problem, not for me," said the friendly major-doctor. "Next!"

An hour later, Patrick stood facing the recruiting officer, Captain J. P. T. Mackesey. The man went over a number of personal questions out loud while Corporal Conway steadily dipped his pen into the ink pot and scratched away, filling an entire sheet of paper. It went quickly, except when Patrick hesitated a moment after he was asked, "Have you ever served in the Royal Navy, the Militia, the Volunteers, etc.?"

Actually, my experience would be an advantage, he suddenly thought.

"Have you ever been in the army?" inquired the captain, scarcely looking up.

"No," Patrick answered reluctantly.

"Put your hand on the Bible," the corporal commanded.

"Repeat after me," began Captain Mackesey. His voice was solemn. "I, John Condon, son of John Condon of Waterford, pledge my allegiance to His Majesty King George the Fifth, to his heirs or successors, and to the generals and officers of his armies."

Totally bewildered, Patrick then had to put his signature down in a space next to his filled-in name. His scribbling looked pitiful in contrast to the graceful letters of the military.

"Of course, there will be a brief examination of possible acquaintances whom we trust," said the captain without looking up. "If no objections arise, you'll be accepted. Soldier six-three-two-two, Private John Condon, congratulations and welcome into the Special Reserve of the Royal Irish Regiment."

"Thank you, sir," said Patrick. He jumped to attention, but the captain and corporal already had their eyes on the doorway.

"Next!"

A Raw Recruit

Patrick succeeded in exchanging a few words with his father that evening after all. When he said that the recruitment process had gone quickly, the man growled an indifferent "I see" to himself. "There never was any real work in soldiering anyhow," he remarked spitefully a bit later.

It grew quieter in the living room. Father spoke to his wife, but his words were meant for his son. "And that pay—it's for us. Understood? The army covers his room and board. Drinking money and other expenses he can scrape together himself. He's cunning enough to do it."

It's one positive note, anyway, Patrick thought. He kept his mouth shut.

❦

Training began in earnest the next day. The scores of recruits who had reported during the past weeks were arranged in long rows in the courtyard of the barracks and put through their first marching paces. It was a ludicrous sight, a disarray of large and small, colorful and gray, hats and caps, long coats and short jackets.

The big difference between this arsenal and the one in Clonmel was the cold, rigid manner of the noncommissioned officers here, to say nothing of the arrogant officers who were totally unapproachable to boys like Patrick. "John" Condon was merely soldier 6322 of the Third Battalion of the Royal Irish Regiment. Period.

For hours at a time, they were shouted at and scolded by tireless drillmasters. If the men made too many mistakes or if their training in marching, saluting, and turning didn't progress quickly enough, the sergeant ordered them to stand at attention, in the rain and the wind, for half the day if need be. Patrick was barely allowed to go home in the first weeks. His only protection against the raging officers was his experience. He never made mistakes, and he let the verbal abuse pass over him like water off a duck's back.

Recruit Condon led a true double life in those days. At the barracks he was "Little John" and eighteen. At home or with friends he was Patrick, a strapping lad of twelve. Only in a big city such as Waterford, or well away from this area, could he keep playing those two roles at the same time.

Occasionally Patrick was allowed to go home for a couple of days, such as at Christmastime and New Year's. Patrick realized that sooner rather than later he'd be sent to a different barracks, far from friends and acquaintances; therefore, he enjoyed every hour at home, where no one asked difficult questions. His relationship with Father remained awkward, but the man spent more time outside the house than inside. Patrick especially found his sister-in-law, Mollie, to be a breath of fresh air. She was much more cheerful and spontaneous than Kate and Margaret, though he had to admit that his sisters relied entirely on Mollie and were slowly blossoming because of her presence. Peter and Mollie's cute little toddler brought a great deal of liveliness to the household and had completely won over the girls— and him. Or was Patrick looking at women and families differently than he used to? His thoughts returned to Moira . . . and to Thomas Carthy and his wife, Mary. And to Roy and the McGuinnesses. How were they doing? He would have to send them all a Christmas card right away.

The World on Fire

Patrick's training in the Special Reserve lasted exactly four months. It was too long for his liking. He could barely wait to be treated as a real military man. And at the end of February 1914, the time had come; his efforts were rewarded and he was placed in the regular army. Soldier 6322, J. Condon, truly belonged to the Third Battalion of the Royal Irish Regiment now. The drillmaster didn't prolong the ceremony in the courtyard any longer than necessary, after which he informed the successful recruits that they would be sent immediately to Clonmel, where the battalion was headquartered. Patrick was looking forward to going. He craved the real soldier's life and longed to see his old friends again. And home? Now that the coziness of the Christmas holidays was past, the house on Wheelbarrow Lane suddenly seemed too small and too snug. He wanted space, an actual life, a return to freedom, which he'd already tasted for a bit. Therefore, saying goodbye to his family wasn't difficult in the least. And although his mother and sisters cried, Father was unflinching.

"At last, Tom!" Patrick lowered his rifle and threw his free arm around Tom's shoulder. "I'm finally back in Clonmel, happy to see you again." He sighed and wrested his arms from the straps of his knapsack, which Tom then took from him.

"Is everything all right with your wife, Tom? Will you give Mrs. Carthy my very best?"

"Everything's okay, thank you. And congratulations, eh? A soldier at last!"

Patrick led his friend aside. "There was no trouble with my unexpected departure from the militia, was there?" he asked anxiously.

"I made sure of that, didn't I? Your resignation was no disaster for Clonmel. And I arranged for your personal items with the quartermaster and the men of the magazine. Just be matter-of-fact about it, and then no one will ask questions. In any case, we have a new colonel and he has other things on his mind besides wanting to shear a runaway sheep."

Tom was right. Old acquaintances in the barracks thought it was fine that Little John had climbed up to the regular troops. No questions were asked; he was accepted. Patrick Condon of Waterford had a new start. He put his past—his boyhood years, his double life—behind him. The world lay open before him. And his permanent name was John Condon now.

AUSTRIAN CROWN PRINCE AND PRINCESS MURDURED

From our correspondent in Sarajevo

Yesterday, 28 June 1914, while visiting the Bosnian capital of Sarajevo, the Austrian crown prince Franz Ferdinand and his consort, Sophie, were shot and killed by a Bosnian nationalist. Earlier that day, the royal couple barely escaped a bomb attack. Their chauffeur was able to accelerate just as the explosive rolled over the roadway, but three people in the following auto were injured. Seven spectators were hurt as well. As they were returning from the hospital, where the prince was visiting the victims, a certain Gavrilo Princip jumped onto the running board of the royal auto and at close range shot His Royal Highness Franz Ferdinand of Austria in the neck. Princess Sophie was struck in the lower belly. Both died at the scene. The perpetrator was immediately overpowered . . .

Thomas Carthy, frowning, folded up the evening paper. "I'm just an ordinary soldier who doesn't know much about politics, but this could well have set off a powder keg."

"You mean war?" asked John Condon, who was next to him on the bench. They were sitting in Tom's garden, enjoying the evening sun with a glass of beer in hand.

Tom didn't answer.

"Sarajevo isn't exactly in our backyard," said John. "Why are you worrying about it?"

"Austria is a good chum of the German Kaiser," replied Tom. "Europe will be too small if those Germans break loose. And don't think that war is a lark. Anyway, it hasn't yet come to that. Besides, you have to be nine-teen to go to the front, soldier boy!"

"One more year!"

"Rookie," said Tom with a laugh.

A month later, on August 4, 1914, Germany invades Belgium. The Germans had figured on a free thorough-fare for attacking France, but it has turned out differently. "Poor little Belgium" is being crushed by "the Hun"—their women are being assaulted, their children murdered. That's what the London politicians and British newspapers are saying about the Germans. Little Belgium must be rescued. Great Britain immediately declares war on Germany. The entire British nation is turned upside down. Because the regular army numbers only 750,000 men, the minister of war, Field Marshal Lord Kitchener, seeks volunteers. He starts a media campaign and has posters created with life-size pictures of himself printed upon them. With his military mustache and military dress, Lord Kitchener addresses each British man threateningly, telling him to do his patriotic duty. "BRITONS, JOIN YOUR COUNTRY'S ARMY." And the minister in the poster points his finger at the reader: "KITCH-

ENER WANTS YOU" or "REMEMBER BELGIUM." Hundreds of thousands of men let themselves be hustled by writers, journalists, schoolteachers, and hired speakers, all of whom urge the masses to join the war effort. Many Irishmen even believe that the English king will grant them true independence after the war if they report in droves to the front. It seems like a romantic adventure, a chance of a lifetime for real fellows, a great picnic for men among men. *We'll be home for Christmas* resounds in all of the English-speaking countries of the world. A healthy man must come up with good reasons not to participate. Besides, the minister has guaranteed each soldier a minimum weekly salary of seven shillings for as long as the war lasts. Many teenagers let themselves be dragged into the fray, too. You must be nineteen to go to the front, but most lie about their age. The recruiting agents merely look the other way.

For John Condon—Patrick, that is—the age problem was solved long ago. He is in the regular army now and is mobilized on August 7, 1914. And just like his oldest army friend, Thomas Carthy, and the rest of the Third Battalion, he would be put through a crash course in preparation for the real fight.

In Dublin's Fair City . . .

The usually quiet army post in the southern Irish town of Clonmel turns into an ants' nest. The barracks look like a fortress of men who are armed to the teeth. Recruits come flocking in without stop, causing the buildings to nearly burst at the seams. Everyone is wound up, as if the enemy were to appear at the gate on that very day. Reports from Belgium and France seep in through the newspapers and are laid on thick. The First Battalion, which conscripted a lot of John and Tom's comrades, is the first to leave. No one knows where it is going. Later they hear that the battalion is fighting with the Tenth Division in Egypt and Palestine.

It's not long before the Third Battalion leaves by train and heads north. John Condon ends up in the vicinity of Dublin, where the Royal Irish Regiment stays in the countless barracks around the capital.

The men receive rigorous training in Dublin. Even so, John has a wonderful time: endless shooting practice in the freezing cold, marching with full packs for hours and hours, man-to-man combat, bayonet practice in which they attack huge straw dummies and heavy jute sacks that are swishing all around . . .

"Look, you have to turn the bayonet around in the damned Hun," says John as he demonstrates to Tom. "Then the wound won't heal." John learned about that from his old drill sergeant.

It's a game for young John as long as sand is spilled, not blood, Thomas Carthy thinks. The forty-six-year-old Irishman secretly hopes that it will remain a game. But such a thought is better kept to oneself.

The British Army hauls the newest weapons out of

the closet. John can't take his eyes off them. Biplanes and triplanes stretch in formation flight above the glowing rocky practice fields and are applauded by the foot soldiers. The pilots, clad in leather caps and goggles, wave to the men on the ground and disappear in their crafts behind the hills surrounding the city.

The regiment receives a demonstration of a gigantic Vickers machine gun. No one has ever seen the likes of it: a fire-spewing monster on a tripod and a water-cooling system to go with it.

"I could win the war all by myself with that," John crows.

Tom shrugs. "You need a whole platoon just to lug that thing along. Besides, *they* have those machine guns, too."

John throws his first grenade into a practice trench. *Get down to the ground, cover your ears, there's a dull bang, the earth shakes . . .* What an experience!

The captain walks approvingly among the crawling troops. Using his cane, he urges those lagging behind to move closer. A strange apparatus is being dragged over the field. The soldiers must come see this new gadget: a grenade launcher. Everyone admires this little machine.

It looks like a portable mini cannon without a barrel. The captain inserts a blank cartridge, slips a whopper of a shell into the holder, and fires. The officer is applauded when the projectile is hurled effortlessly a hundred yards into the air.

"Those Fritzes don't stand a ghost of a chance, Tom!"

"The Germans weren't born yesterday. Their steel factories have been going at full speed in preparation for war," Tom says grimly.

❧

In spite of the difficult military maneuvers, there is time for other activities, such as the compulsory afternoon review of troops for all those who don't have to crawl over the rocky practice fields of Dublin. It's a matter of hammering in the right spirit and discipline. Lieutenant Edmunds conducts his inspection and remains standing by John.

"Name?"

"Soldier Condon, John, number six-three-two-two, *sir!*"

"Sergeant-Major Lewis, make sure that this dirty sod

gets his just punishment. Face isn't washed, hands are dirty, shoes are filthy."

John receives four days' confinement to his quarters. He must remain in the barrack during his free time. It's quite a blow, certainly now that groups of soldiers are allowed to spend an afternoon in the city.

"In Dublin's fair city, where girls are so pretty, I first set my eyes on sweet Mollie Malone . . ." All the men are singing and laughing at him as they leave the barrack. Disillusioned, John remains behind. He has lots of cleaning up to do.

When the sergeant-major conducts his inspection rounds an hour later, he finds that soldier 6322 is not in his room in the barrack. After two hours, John is back again. Lieutenant-Colonel Kavenagh gives him a proper dressing-down. "Where have you been? Taking a walk, perhaps? Condon, do you realize what you're risking? Desertion! And that carries the death penalty! This is war, man!"

"I'm sorry, sir," John says, trying to excuse himself. He comes off with a doubling of his punishment.

Just before dusk, his comrades return from Dublin. He can hear them singing in the distance: ". . . through the streets broad and narrow, singing cockles and mussels alive, alive-oh!"

That same month, November 1914, a few hundred men of the Second Battalion leave for an unknown destination. The excitement in the camps is great. Of course everyone knows that they'll be sent to the front in France. Most likely everyone has heard, too, that this same battalion was as good as annihilated during the very first battles, when the advancing Germans flattened "poor little Belgium." No one really wants to listen to those stories of their predecessors. Intensely jealous, John walks among the men of the Second Battalion and tastes the excitement that rises above their conversations.

"Are you coming with us, boy?" they shout, half drunk.

"I would if I could, and right away!"

There is promising news on December 16. John and Tom's platoon is transferred from the Third Battalion to the Second. For the first time in months, John spends his evening drinking a couple of bottles of beer.

To his surprise, he meets his former neighbor from Waterford, Michael Mahoney, who has just arrived. He's in the Second Battalion, too.

"Hey, Patrick!" Mahoney calls. "So here you are, you brat!"

John gestures for him to be quiet.

Mahoney chuckles. "Sorry. 'John' is what I should say. You don't have to explain to me, lad. Our whole street knows about it anyway. And I can keep a secret."

It is already late in the evening. John is searching for his bed, his mind a blur after all the beer. "We're finally moving up, Tom." He is rattling on like a crazy alarm clock to his mate. "When the Royal Irish Regiment sends troops again, they'll almost certainly come from the Second Battalion! It'll be our turn then."

Thomas Carthy knows all too well why the Second Battalion needs fresh troops. At the front they are dying at an alarming rate. He grabs John just before he tumbles out of his bed.

The Last Christmas

The Second Battalion is clearly under the war's spell. The practice fights are harder and fiercer. Everyone in Dublin is trained and motivated and looking forward to the real confrontation with the enemy. The men expect each day to be *the* day, but they are kept hanging in the air. In their euphoric moments they show off for one another and say how much they would like to run a bayonet through a Fritz. When the battalion unexpectedly returns to Clonmel right before Christmas, the reactions are mixed. There is disillusionment, but relief too. A break is welcome.

Whoever lives nearby is allowed to leave the ever-crowded barracks. Tom has his wife and tiny cottage. John has his second home and his horses at the farm. He can't return to Waterford because it's too far. For the first time, he spends Christmas Eve without his family. Never before has he so missed the people of Wheelbarrow Lane. The holiday always used to be something special. Usually they stayed up extra late at home, drank a glass of whiskey, then left together to celebrate midnight mass at the parish church of St. Patrick of the Holy Trinity Without. John even misses his friends tonight. He doesn't want to bother Thomas Carthy and his wife, and the McGuinnesses are having their family over at the farm. Even Roy has gone out. Although John isn't on duty, he hangs around in the barrack for a while, chatting with the unlucky soldiers who must keep watch. He finally kills time in his room with a book of maps. The ticking of the clock on the wall is exasperatingly noisy and slow. At half past eleven he takes his jacket and cap from the clothes peg and heads for the church. He is one of the first to arrive, but by midnight the nave is full. All the faces are those of strangers. He thinks about what is to come—the front, the trenches that the men have been talking about every now and then. John is longing to go. He sees his frozen breath evaporating in the weak gaslight. The church radiates something very special: the living crib, the smell of the ox and the donkey, the thin voices of angels that reverberate high against the rafters, the centuries-old Celtic songs, and especially the darkness, the mystique of this nighttime service.

John can't take his eyes off the living figure of Mary. Is it his imagination? An omen? She looks exactly like his mother. Most people call her Mary, too, even though her real name is Catherine.

❦

John goes calling on the Carthys on Christmas Day. Mary answers the door.

"Ah, the young Condon!" she exclaims. The reunion is cordial, but John immediately notices that the woman is trying to hide her anxiety.

"I've come to get Tom. We have to be back at the barracks in an hour."

She nods and lets him in. "We have a visitor," she says. "He's just returned from the front." She points to a tall, thin soldier at the table. He is sitting with his back toward John.

"Jim, this is the boy I was talking about," Tom says. He motions for John to take a seat.

"My cousin Jim was wounded in Belgium," Tom continues. "He's in the Second Battalion."

John feels his heart begin to beat faster. A real soldier at the front, someone who has seen the war! *Really?* he almost calls out.

The man remains motionless. John would like to shake his hand, but stiffens when the stranger finally turns around. His right eye has been crudely sewn shut. Pink babylike skin is stretched over the area that was once his cheek. It's full of little wrinkles.

"Hi, John," says the man, breaking the silence. He raises his right arm, which is half gone. "Sorry, the rest of it is in Belgium." He extends his left hand now.

John stares at the deformed face in shocked silence. This is not at all what a war hero should look like . . .

The humming of the stove fills the quiet room.

"He was allowed to leave the hospital for a little bit

because it's Christmas," says Tom, trying to keep the conversation going.

"Do take a seat," Mrs. Carthy says to John. She sniffles.

A bottle of whiskey is on the table. Cousin Jim refills his glass and tells how they eagerly set foot in the French harbor city of Boulogne in August. Together with the BEF—British Expeditionary Force—they were the first to enter Belgium. Near Mons, their battalion was wiped off the map just as quickly as the Belgian troops were.

"It was terrible," Jim continues. "Those first deaths don't seem real. You can't believe it. Until you search for your best friends and find them without arms or legs or even heads." He gulps down his whiskey and gropes awkwardly for a handkerchief.

"Quiet, Jim," says Mrs. Carthy, trying to soothe him. "You don't have to talk about all this."

"I've got to," he answers aggressively. "Otherwise . . . otherwise . . ."

"Was that your last battle?" asks John. The others are startled, because the boy hasn't spoken until now.

"My last was a few weeks afterward, at Le Pilly."

Jim searches for words. In fits and starts, he tells how

the Second Battalion, to which John and Tom now belong, had to compete against the superior strength of German cannons and infantry. It was pure suicide. Major Daniell led a greatly depleted battalion of 17 officers and 561 Irish boys. After the last, useless bayonet attack, with Daniell at the head, half the men lay dead and the other half were taken prisoner. Most were seriously wounded. Only thirty boys got away. Everyone thought that Jim was dead, but he ended up in a field hospital. That's where his eye was removed. His arm had to be amputated two days later.

"Home before Christmas!" Jim mutters cynically. He's a bit drunk. "Somehow I had imagined that this Great Picnic would be different."

Away at Last

John is not allowed to leave the barracks once the news of their departure is confirmed. Tom enters the room, where everyone is busy packing. He looks as though he has aged five years. John doesn't dare ask what saying farewell to Mrs. Carthy was like.

As they march out of the barracks a few hours later, a mass of spectators is standing at the gate. The military police do almost nothing to separate the throng from the soldiers.

"John! Tom!" A faraway voice rises above the turmoil.

"Over there." Tom points with little enthusiasm. He forces a smile.

"Hey, Roy!" John notices the farm hand, who pushes his way forward.

Roy hands John a small linen sack. "Blood pudding for your journey!" he calls excitedly. A burly MP grabs him by the collar.

"The others have come, too! Over there!" Roy adds. He is shoved back.

A little farther, in the third and fourth rows of people, John can just catch a glimpse of Paul and Sinead McGuinness waving and shouting enthusiastically. Moira is standing next to them. She raises her hand and waves hesitantly.

"We'll get those Krauts!" John shouts. His voice is cracking, but no one can hear it above the noise.

John would like to forget the boat trip to France as quickly as possible. If the rocking and rolling doesn't do you in, you might well be sick as a dog from the stink of vomit in the overcrowded hold. Getting a bit of fresh air up on deck is no comfort, for there is always someone retching over the rails. John feels his best when he's with the horses. There must be a hundred of them stabled in the forecastle: splendid mounts as well as hefty farm animals, all requisitioned by the army, all taken from their quiet villages in Great Britain and lugged over the Channel to the front.

The battalion moves in long rows through the busy harbor of Boulogne-sur-Mer. The men march to the singsong music of three flutes and a couple of drums as they proceed in the direction of the station. John can see a terrified stallion being lifted onto the wharf by an enormous crane. His attention quickly shifts to the green banners that stand out above the bobbing of military caps. Here come the Irish, and those French "Frogs" and English "Tommies" need to know about it. John, who for many is the mascot of the Second Battalion, is handed a green-colored banner, too. He has yet to receive his baptism by fire, but already he feels like a true hero now.

"The ragamuffins of Ballybricken should see me here, Mike!" he cries to Michael Mahoney, his former neighbor on Wheelbarrow Lane.

"Condon! Keep your pace!" a sergeant admonishes him.

John does a one-two skip and falls back in cadence. Way in the distance, he can see the battalion commander, Colonel Moriarty, leading the procession on horseback.

🦋

An unbelievably long train takes them eastward into France, almost to the Belgian border. For the time being, they end up in Rue de Bois, a little place in northern France, where they pitch their tents. It is teeming with green banners and ribbons, for other Irish newcomers have arrived. The Second Battalion Royal Munster Fusiliers are billeted here, too. Before they have fired a single shot, John, Tom, and their mates spend an evening of uproarious fraternizing. They are treated to strong drink, stronger stories, lewd songs, and even a little concert.

"This war isn't half bad!" John screams above the noise to Tom. "Here, this rum is for you. Much too strong for me!"

"Cheers!" Tom answers. "Santé, mademoiselle!" He has already had enough to drink. He laughs himself silly as he watches the sketches of the men dressed in women's clothes on the improvised podium.

"Do all women have those mustaches here?" a jokester asks during a momentary lull. Laughter erupts once more, and the veteran soldiers begin to sing again:

If the sergeant steals your rum, never mind.
If the sergeant steals your rum, never mind.
Know he's just a bloody sot;
Let him take the bleeding lot.
If the sergeant steals your rum, never mind.

A hundred men join in with each "never mind." Their shouts fill the tent. And the text grows lewder by the stanza.

The next day, reports are seeping through that units of the British Expeditionary Force have been ground into mincemeat at Neuve-Chapelle. John listens in surprise to the gruesome testimonies about the German barbed wire in northern France. He hears about the wounded boys, entangled for days, who were finally finished off. The British professional army was already greatly depleted six months ago at the Battle of Ypres. Now there is hardly anyone left.

John doesn't let himself become discouraged, however. *They won't trifle with us,* he thinks. Instead, he lets himself be carried away by those crazy marching songs as they stride toward the Belgian border. Only the men who have already been to the front know that they are singing in order to forget.

Mademoiselle from Armenteers, parlez-vous.
Your pommes de terre frites
They give us the squits.
Inky pinky parlez-vous . . .

A few hours later, these same men who were trying to outdo one another with their most vulgar of verses are on their knees in prayer. They're Irish soldiers, all of them, from different battalions. Green pennants are fluttering everywhere, for the men are proud of their heritage. There is talk again about Irish independence. "We can finally fight for it here," John hears someone say. "We'll let the English king see what we're worth."

The men are quiet as mice when Father Gleeson, the padre of the regiment, presides over the hundreds of bowed, bared heads. From high on horseback he offers his blessings and forgives each man his sins. Afterward, a resounding hymn rises to the sky: "Hail, Queen of Heaven!" The Virgin Mary effortlessly takes the spotlight from the Mademoiselle of Armenteers. Here and there a soldier brushes away a tear.

After prayers, the men swarm back to the encampment. Their voices are subdued. There is high tension in the air, an indescribable feeling of solidarity. Thomas Carthy is daydreaming, staring in the direction of the chaplain. The padre is folding up his portable altar and lashing it to his horse.

"Tom! Are you coming?" John calls.

His friend doesn't answer; he is lost in thought. John goes over and pulls on his sleeve.

"Oh," Tom says, startled. "Just a moment."

"Is something wrong?" John asks.

Tom shrugs. He has a faraway look in his eyes. "I think things will soon be getting serious here, John."

"Yes, I hope so, too."

Tom looks at his young friend and shakes his head. "You go ahead. I'll be along shortly."

John walks toward the camp. When he looks back, he sees his friend talking to Father Gleeson.

Soldiers in All Colors

Their battalion approaches the French-Belgian border. The soldiers spend the nights on farms; the first winter months of 1915 are cold and harsh. In the lost hours, John's comrades take silly pleasure in a pocket book called *French Lessons*. Reading does nothing for John. His head is full of anticipation of the war. Most of the men have other adventures on their minds—perhaps they can nab a French girl!

"Bone-jure, mademwezel. Como tolly voo?"

But when the farmer's daughter pokes her head around the barn door a little later, no one can utter a single word.

John has absolutely no knowledge of this area. He's aware that he's in France, of course, but France is a big country. They spend two days near the Katsberg, in a little place called Godewaersvelde. Because the British are unable to pronounce the name, they say "Gertie wears velvet." *It's such a pretty name for a French town—I'll have to remember it,* John thinks.

The battalion marches into Belgium that same week. They continue to proceed to Poperinge, a garrison city behind the frontlines. All soldiers are sent to the battlefield from "Pops"—first to Ypres, from where they will spread out over the surrounding villages and glowing landscape and take their positions. If they're lucky, they will return via Ypres to Poperinge.

The front has remained stationary these past few months. All the troops have dug themselves into trenches that stretch for kilometers. Some are only a few dozen meters from the enemy. A stubborn battle is being waged around Ypres. The Germans have moved their artillery to the tops of hills surrounding the city and beyond, where they can easily keep the French and British positions in range of their cannons and howitzers. The frontline runs diagonally across the map of Europe, from the north at Nieuwpoort by the North Sea down to Switzerland in the southeast. The line makes a marked bulge in the vicinity of Ypres; the British call this the "Ypres Salient." It is here in the thick clay that the horrifying history of the war is being written with the blood of hundreds of thousands of young men.

The icy wind rips into John's face. He pushes his cap farther down over his dark hair. The straps of the leaden rucksack dig into his shoulders. He must support his rifle with both hands. The hilly country roads, with their dangerously slick cobblestones, make marching difficult. All the men are complaining about their aching feet. John can see Poperinge in the distance. Just before they approach the first houses, they pass a farm with enormous Red Cross tents everywhere. Even though it's freezing, scores of soldiers are lying on stretchers outside. It slowly occurs to John that these are fresh corpses. This realization of death casts a shadow over the battalion as it marches by. The buzzing of voices stops; there is only the stark cadence of hundreds of boots on the cobblestones. Nurses walk in and out of the tents in silence. John sees two doctors in a heated discussion as they walk across the grounds to the field hospital. He hears fragments of English. Their white aprons are covered with blood. A long, piercing scream is coming from a hospital tent. John and his mates look around. The doctors don't react; they are lighting cigars.

❦

A half hour later, the Second Battalion Royal Irish Regiment marches between the tall row houses of the Gasthuisstraat. Cafés and driveways are everywhere, and the local citizens and military personnel go in and out of them like bees swarming around a hive. The Irish turn up at the Grote Markt. It looks like a carnival. When the long rows of steaming bodies finally come to a halt, John hears a buzzing among the masses of spectators, who are curious about the new arrivals. Everyone calls out to John and his buddies; perhaps they have news from the motherland.

The men begin to joke with a group of Scottish soldiers. "It's some weather for a kilt, eh, Mac?" Michael Mahoney shouts.

"It's a good thing there's whiskey to warm you up," another Irishman adds with a laugh.

"But where would he keep his flask?" yells another.

One Scot takes off his plaid cap and raises his fists. His comrades calm him down and lead him away. As they depart, another Scot lifts his kilt defiantly and moons the Irish company. All the soldiers go crazy now and roar with laughter. The highlander is treated to catcalls.

"Look there," Thomas Carthy says a bit later. He points.

Everyone looks around. "Blacks!" they shout together.

A group of Senegalese soldiers in black-blue uniforms are shivering in the cold and watch the Irish from a distance. They have bright red fezzes on their heads.

"What are those fellows doing here?" John asks his friend. He has never seen a black man before, like most Irishmen.

"They're West African troops from the French colonies. Troops from our colonies are here, too."

A few hours later, after everyone has found a place to sleep in an old factory, John and Tom go into the city. There are drinking houses galore, one smoky café after another. The citizens of Poperinge are earning good money from the war. There's no shortage of women, either. John stares in disbelief at mothers who turn a blind eye and allow their young daughters to be manhandled by grabby Tommies.

"As long as the soldiers pay," Tom says grumpily from his chair in a café. "In cash!"

Africans pass by the café without entering. John gazes at them through the window.

Money is spent freely indeed. Tom and John fall into conversation with a very tipsy Welshman. He drivels on about life and death in garbled English.

"Tomorrow could well be the end. Have a drink on me, Irishmen."

Tom begins to rise, but the man pushes him back into his chair.

"Wait a minute," John presses on. "I want to hear about Ypres."

"Ypres? Pretty town!" the man says, slurring his words. "Walls weren't enough for them. Now they have trenches, too, and they let them fill up with blood. *Our* blood!"

Both the Welshman and the men of the Second Battalion will be moving to the front tomorrow. The drunken soldier has obviously not spent all his money. He raises three fingers and motions to the hostess at the bar. She worms her way through the packed house and sets three bottles down on the table. The Welshman hands her money and lets her keep the change—for a kiss, of course.

Tom and John quickly drink their beer and rid themselves of the man. They walk through the town. Glowing cigarette tips dance like fireflies in the evening. Soldiers are standing around in the streets, waiting to shuffle into the half-darkened pubs. The officers slip in through their own entrances. Each uniformed man is living in the whirl of his very last evening, the night before Judgment Day.

"Those men are from *our* colonies," Tom whispers.

"Turbans!"

"Shh!"

John puts his hand over his mouth. What a fascinating city Poperinge is for a thirteen-year-old street kid! A group of five Sikhs from British India walks past. They have dark skin and enormous beards. John steps back to get a better look.

Queue to the Front

Spirits are high as the Second Battalion Royal Irish Regiment travels by train via Vlamertinge to Ypres. It feels like they're going at a snail's pace, for John, Tom, and their company are standing shoulder to shoulder in open cars and it's freezing cold. They wave with their caps and call to the passersby. The French troops, clad in red knickers and tall, round caps, are attracting attention in the distance. The French lessons from the communal book come in handy again for the Irish, for they help maintain the atmosphere during the trip.

The train comes to a halt at the western edge of Ypres. Everyone gets off and lines up for inspection of the new khaki uniform. Each has black shoes, green puttees that reach to just below the knee, and a thick winter coat. On top of the coat is a leather harness consisting of a pistol belt around the middle, with two bands rising straight over the shoulders. On the back is a flat rucksack; on the left hip, a pouch and a bayonet in its scabbard. The corporals and sergeants distribute the personal ammunition. On each side of the breast pocket are five leather cartridge holders mounted on the belts. The ten little bags are filled with bullets. There is one last inspection of the rifle. Everyone is ready now. Ready for what? No one knows.

They march across the city wall and enter the center of Ypres through the Lille Gate. Now and then a cannon rumbles in the distance. After almost six months of war, the medieval center bears grievous traces of the German artillery. To the left and right are big gaping holes in the rows of houses.

"It's such a shame," Tom says with a sigh when they make a right turn toward the market.

"Wow! What a town hall!" John calls. He points to a tall building on his left. It is one hundred fifty meters long. The roof and entire pieces of the impressive façade have been blown to bits.

"That must be the Cloth Hall," says Tom. He knows all about this building and its fate because back in Ireland he faithfully read the reports from the front in his newspaper. "Look there—the Bell Tower. God, what destruction. Centuries of history in ruins!"

"Over there you can see a church through the rubble." John points excitedly to the cathedral behind the Bell Tower, next to the Cloth Hall. He feels that the real war, the adventure that he has anticipated for such a long time, is no longer far away. What he doesn't realize is that just four or five kilometers from the Grote Markt are the British and French trenches. They form a crescent-shaped frontline encompassing the eastern edge of Ypres. A few dozen meters farther—and sometimes just a few meters farther—are the Germans, positioned and waiting to capture the city.

At about five o'clock, the winter sun begins to sink behind the Cloth Hall. The battalion prepares to move through the Menin Gate to the trenches. The market square is teeming with soldiers; some are waiting impatiently while others are marching by. Before departing, Colonel Moriarty inspects his troops once again. He boosts their morale in a short, moving speech. It is obvious that he too is nervous, and curious about what awaits them. When he walks past John, who is a bit smaller than most of the others, he pats him approvingly on the back and straightens one of his shoulder bands. John turns all warm inside. He can see that parade on the wharf at Boulogne again and the image of the colonel triumphantly leading his troops on horseback. *I'll go through hell for this man,* he thinks.

The Menin Gate appears to be a gap in the old star-shaped walls of defense that Vauban, Louis XIV's architect, once had erected around Ypres. The road that begins just beyond the city wall—Menin Road—is wide and quite busy. Citizens and soldiers enter and exit the city in carts and on horseback. Troops from all corners of the earth come and go. And according to tradition, there is always a group of British spectators calling to the departing soldiers, "Will the last person to leave shut the gate?"

After two hundred and fifty meters, the Menin Road

turns sharply to the right. It is here that the route to the front truly begins. The battalion ends up in a queue. The hundreds of Irish shuffle forward inch by inch. In the meantime, it is growing pitch-dark. A few men light lanterns. They wait, smoke, and grumble because their progress is so slow. Suddenly the traffic from the other direction is noticeably busier.

"Where are they all coming from?" John wonders aloud.

"Where do you think?" Tom replies. "From the trenches, of course. They had to wait until dark before returning."

In the dim lamplight, the Irish get a better look at the weary faces of these approaching soldiers. The first march past silently in their platoons. They are followed—much more slowly—by ragtag groups of four or five men. Some walk all alone. No one reacts to the questions asked by the fresh troops. Drivers shout "Move aside!" and maneuver their horse carts with ghastly precision over the heavily traveled Menin Road.

"Poor sods," whisper a few men behind John and Tom.

"What do you mean?" John asks.

"Didn't you just see that, little man?" says Michael

Mahoney. "Let's hope they won't be sending *you* back like that tomorrow, Condon."

"Dead bodies were in those carts," says Sergeant Kelly, who is passing them as he walks to the front of the line. His voice is shaky and hoarse.

John and Tom are about to reply when a motorized ambulance with its lights off emerges from the darkness. Furious shouting and a heart-rending call for help rise above the noise of the vehicle.

"Some wish that they were dead, too," growls an MP—a military police officer—who is standing nearby and directing traffic. "But you don't have a choice out there. An arm, a leg . . . you can't place your order with the Fritzes." He pushes the Irish to the side. "Look out, here comes another ambulance. Out of the way!" he calls, waving a lamp.

The soldiers keep coming. Some are limping along, supported by their comrades. Others are wrapped in bandages. They all appear equally filthy and bedraggled.

Suddenly there seem to be many more MPs on the scene. "From here on, all lights and lanterns must be put out!" shouts one in a gruff and commanding voice.

Everyone is startled by the unexpected order, but

within two seconds the entire battalion is engulfed in silence and darkness. Each person holds his tongue and waits.

"You might well ask why *I'm* not putting out my lantern," the raspy voice continues. "That's because we're still standing between houses. A little farther up there's nothing more, not even a tree to pee against, because most have already been destroyed."

"What an animal," John whispers to Tom.

"A blessing for his wife that there's a war on," Michael Mahoney adds scornfully.

The blunt MP comes forward and stops in front of Michael. "Can *you* explain it better than I?" he snaps. "No? Move along, then!"

John holds his breath. Michael looks down at his toes. The storm blew over.

"If you want the Krauts to aim a shell between your legs, put your light back on," the MP continues. "Or do you want to lose the tip of your nose? Then light a cigarette."

"So no smoking?" Sergeant Kelly asks.

"Right, Sergeant! Lights out, cigarettes away. Whoever doesn't want to obey my command will soon suffer the consequences. We don't want the whole battalion blown into the air before you've seen the front. It would be a terrible waste of your travel expenses. Orders to cross at Hellfire Corner will be given by our officers immediately."

Hellfire Corner: Green Light for Screaming Horses

Hellfire Corner is one and one and a half kilometers from the Menin Gate, yet Colonel Moriarty's Irish battalion takes hours to reach it. For John, Tom, and their comrades, it means waiting in line amid the other troops and dozens of carts and horses. Crossing this junction is something else again, however, for Hellfire Corner is generally considered to be the most dangerous place on earth. The front is just straight up ahead along the road to Menin—not even a five-minute walk to the first trench. But the railway to Zonnebeke and Roeselare cuts diagonally across the way here, and the cobblestone road to Zillebeke traverses this point, too. From on top of the Frezenberg and the Bellewaarde Ridge, the Germans follow every movement with eagle eyes. The far-off hills and windmills serve as observation posts as well. Almost all British and French troops must be funneled through this dreaded intersection to the front, and if they survive, they must return along the same route.

In addition to watching the movements of the troops here, the Germans also keep an eye on the railway traffic. In clear weather they monitor the surroundings from small anchored zeppelins. The crucial delivery of ammunition and food for the many thousands of soldiers in the trenches must cross Hellfire Corner, too. At first these supplies are shipped by night trains, then by horse and cart because it is safer. Intersections like Hellfire Corner are notated on every topographic map, including German ones. Poor visibility or darkness of night are not problems for the German gunners; they are true wizards at geometry, and though they might have to move their artillery every now and then, they can easily land their shellfire in the area of the pitch-dark traffic junction.

"You're in luck tonight. It hasn't been this quiet in weeks," calls an unfamiliar officer who has come to brief the Irish.

"Downright quiet—you can say that again." John snickers as he looks at the swarms of people, horses, and carts.

"From here you must manage to reach the following intersection, Birr Crossroads. There you'll duck down into the trenches, which will be on your left and right. These are your frontline positions. Birr Crossroads is no farther than one hundred fifty yards from here."

"Simple—a stone's throw away," John mutters to Tom.

"Be quiet!" Tom hisses.

"*But!*" the officer continues. He seems to be enjoying the anxiety displayed by the newcomers, and pauses carefully to add weight to his words. "But . . . these one hundred fifty yards could also be your last. When the red lanterns are extinguished, sit as quiet as mice. Then wait for the green light, and be ready for the race of your life. In total darkness. The only things you'll see are our signalers, unless a shell comes overhead. These signalers are situated on both sides of this part of the road, deep down in the ditches, with their backs to the east, to the enemy. And remember: keep to the left, for there could be traffic coming from the other direction."

The instructor has barely finished his sentence when there are frantic cries of "Down! Shellfire!"

Everyone plops face-down, just as the troops so often did in their practice drills. With his nose to the ground and his ears pricked, John can hear the fear spreading over the road. Horses are neighing in front and in back of him, as drivers swear at the snorting animals. Farther away, somewhere above the dreaded one hundred fifty yards, three or four whistling shells skim overhead. The whizzbangs come buzzing down into the fields next to the road. Mules balk in terror, and the horses seem to be screaming. John looks in the direction of the explosions. The half-frozen ground shakes under his pounding heart. When the explosives land, they act as spotlights. He finds it exciting to see clumps of earth flung up high in the flashing light. A horse bolts next to the road, dragging its harness as it runs into the fields. It is only now that John can get a picture of what this intersection actually looks like. The chaos and the masses of people and animals surprise him more than anything else.

When it's far into the night, the battalion readies itself for the big leap. First the men wait for the Royal Engineers, who have to repair the railway line that's been damaged by German shells. They fill in a small hole next to the tracks, then replace a few splintered ties and a bent rail—not more than an hour and a half of work. In the meantime, the Irish make way for a sea of soldiers returning from the trenches. John and Tom are now standing in the front of the line. Even after hours of waiting, their eyes are not used to the pitch-dark. The only points of light are the first covered red lanterns of the signalers. Their company is lined up behind a transport unit. The convoy consists of about five pairs of horses; one pair is pulling a hooded cart, and the others are hitched to flat wagons. John noticed this when the last shell struck. Each team of horses has one driver, who sits astride one animal while holding the reins of the other. The horses snort restlessly. Everyone's patience is being tested—the animals' patience, too.

Suddenly it is quiet. John turns around and looks for the lights. They are gone.

"The time has come," Tom says, and he sighs.

"Ready for the green light?" calls a grim voice somewhere in front of them.

Nothing happens. John makes sure his shoulder bands are in place and pushes his cap way down over his ears. And waits . . .

Green light. "Go! Go, go, go!" Sergeant Kelly shouts. "Yeah! Come on!" the teamsters yell, and they dig their heels into the horses' flanks. The animals rear up and whinny. The carts rattle and creak as they lunge forward. Slowly they gain speed. At first, John and his friends run effortlessly along with one hand on a tailgate. They must let go of the wagon ten seconds later, for the convoy starts moving much too fast for them now. The iron wheels clang over the sloping train tracks and ties in the middle of Hellfire Corner. John follows on the far left of the road and passes four or five signalers hunkered down along the side. Then he himself can feel the slippery girders and tracks of the grade crossing. He knows that Tom is somewhere next to him. Three lights further, there is a resounding boom; it sounds as though lightning has struck right next to John. For two seconds the junction is engulfed in a glaring light. He is hurled to the ground. There is a second flash and a third. John can't hear anything now. A horse lies in front of him; its hind legs are shattered and its intestines are spilling out of its belly. The animal is trying to scramble to its feet. Two boots protrude from under its body. A wheel dances over the road. At that moment, ten men or more jump out of a ditch and drag away the wreckage—cadavers, wounded men, and injured horses. The road must be kept open and clear. John stumbles ahead as fast as he can. His ears are buzzing now; he can hear all the racket again and he can hear voices, including Tom's. He is driven along with the others to Birr Crossroads. Two minutes later, he's catching his breath in a long trench. This is the front. This is the war.

War Is a Frightful Routine

All the Irish have survived the first trip to the front.

"A lucky coincidence," say those in the First Battalion King's Own, who are catching their breath behind the weakly lit rampart at Birr Crossroads before making the perilous journey back to Ypres.

"Just call it a big fluke," one signaler says. "I've already seen hundreds of bleeding boys being carried away. I didn't believe hell existed until I arrived on this spot, but I know where to find it now. From here to Hellfire Corner . . ."

John Condon's group leaves via the trenches in the back line of defense to the north of the front bow. Over a maze of small, deeply dug paths, they walk a few kilometers along the Salient, the defense bow around Ypres. Gradually they move over to the right to the dangerous exterior, where the front trenches form the winding frontline. Long silences are broken by nasty machine-gun fire. Sometimes the guns are far away and at other times perplexingly close. The jet-black sky is regularly illuminated by exploding shells. Iron splinters whiz through the air.

They come across other army units on their grim walk. Some have been there for days and are stiff from the cold. Most of the men are silent. Others sullenly shoot a few bullets over the parapet or between the sandbags. Twice John and his mates have to leave the trench to move faster to the front positions. Shots are fired; John and Tom don't know who is doing the shooting. Scared to death, they hunker down and follow the little white ribbons that point the way. Thanks to an experienced guide, they find the holes in the barbed wire, which is everywhere to be seen.

At daybreak, they learn that they are now in the area of Het Wieltje. The sergeants are taken aside and given orders from the officers. John can't take his eyes off Colonel Moriarty. The man truly radiates charm and charisma! Tom thinks that the colonel cuts an unusually fine figure for an officer as well.

They spend the first day settling in. The greatest enemy seems to be the winter cold. John is swathed in thick clothing, but it's a struggle to keep the feet warm on the duckboards. Whoever continues to walk on the sticky clay makes a filthy mess indeed.

"Above all, keep your feet dry," the sergeant warns.

Each soldier in John's group is given a little jar of grease. "It's made from whale oil," the sergeant adds.

"What are we supposed to do with this, Sergeant?" Michael Mahoney asks.

"Smear it on your feet, honey, all the way up past your shoes," says the man, and he snickers.

John opens his jar and sniffs. "Ugh! That's worse than cod-liver oil!"

"It'll keep you dry. According to the colonel, the army is losing too many men to frostbitten toes."

The Irish take turns watching for the enemy. In the meantime, those not on lookout duty play cards, smoke, drink rum, and tell jokes. A shot rings out only every now and then. Usually someone shoots back. They are so close to the enemy that sometimes they hear German songs. The war seems like a game on that first morning. But before the day is over, John knows that he is horribly mistaken.

"Is there something to see across the way, Murph?" Tom asks.

Murphy, who is on lookout duty, doesn't answer. When Tom nudges him and asks the same question two minutes later, Murphy collapses, falling backwards. He lies next to John's feet and stares at the gray snow clouds, not saying a word. Dark red blood oozes out of his nose and mouth. There is a small hole above one of his eyebrows.

They quickly send for Lieutenant Fottrell. "Sniper," he says when he arrives, and he sighs.

"That fellow never did anyone any harm," John says to himself, dazed.

"Damned snipers," the officer hisses. "Men, don't stick your head over the wall unnecessarily."

"But . . . he had to, didn't he . . . ?" Tom says hesitantly.

"Sergeant!" Lieutenant Fottrell calls. "Have the poor sod removed. Has anyone taken his place yet?"

A second victim falls fifteen minutes later. A jolly platoon that John and his buddies have come to relieve is returning from the field kitchen. The men know nothing about the shooting. A tall soldier named Dobson is clowning around as always. Everyone laughs when he sinks to his knees, until they notice that he is taking a very, very long time to get up. He's been shot through his cap.

From that day on, the fear of snipers holds everyone in its grip. It will remain a burden in the coming weeks and months as well. Every move the soldiers make in the narrow trench weighs on them like a rucksack full of bricks.

The two unlucky soldiers are buried that same afternoon. Nearby is a small snow-covered lot, where already about a hundred wooden crosses are standing. Father Gleeson's short service makes a deep impression on John and the platoon to which the fallen soldiers belonged. Black spots indicate where the fresh graves lie.

A little later, John and Tom are sent with about ten others three kilometers farther up, along the road from Ypres to Pilkem, to fetch sacks of coal. Not only are the lumps of coal used for cooking; they are especially needed to fill the scuttles that help keep the men warm. On the way back, John notices more patches of ground covered with crosses. One plot contains large holes from a recent shelling. Two men silently drag a uniformed torso and return the legless body to its grave, which is now a crater. In the hole lies another body, half naked, half buried.

John sets down his sack of coal.

"Is something wrong?" Tom asks.

"That . . . that was a lieutenant," John stammers. "There was a gold star on his epaulet."

Then he vomits.

The Second Battalion Royal Irish Regiment sets up camp in the area of De Brieke, a hamlet a bit north of Ypres. Just as on typical days in the trenches, not much is happening there. The brick buildings that are still standing have been deserted. Officers take over the best lodgings in safe cellars; then the noncommissioned officers choose their spots. Corporals get the ramshackle remains. Ordinary boys like John must try to keep warm and dry in drafty sheds, barracks, and army tents, where they spread out their bedding on some straw.

Every four days, John and his platoon are sent to the frontline. They remain there for four days and nights before returning to De Brieke, where they spend their time resting and doing odd jobs. And so it goes, week after week.

"Why did we train so hard in Ireland?" John wonders aloud. "Nothing is happening."

Tom puts a pipe in his mouth and checks to see if any of his superiors are around the corner of the trench. "To be honest, lad, I hope it stays that way," he says.

Michael Mahoney leans against the sandbags and looks out through a split every so often. "John is right. The place is dead, Tom. If it were summer, we could be lying in the sun now!"

"I'm afraid this isn't going to be a picnic, Michael."

"I thought we were going to teach those Huns a lesson," John complains.

"Teach them a lesson?" Tom snickers. "Remember my cousin Jim?"

"Christmas at your house," John recalls. "Poor man."

"What about him?" Michael wants to know.

"Oh, you're aware of those gruesome stories that Kinsella and Driscoll tell, aren't you?" Tom says with distaste. "It was really one of the first battles the British troops were involved with in this war. Most of them were ground into mincemeat by the Germans." Michael listens and nods.

"Yup," Tom says with a frown as he puffs away on his pipe. "That was last year, when they were the first to be sent to France and Belgium."

"Do you mean we can't beat those Fritzes?" John calls. He looks rather silly as he jumps up and grabs his rifle.

"You need a fresh diaper?" Michael Mahoney says, laughing as he remembers when John was a toddler and still called Patrick.

"The front isn't moving and we're shooting a few bullets back and forth, but who is going to teach whom a lesson when all hell truly breaks loose here?" Tom asks.

The days and nights in the trenches are long and cold, with little movement at the front. Officers and sergeants make up all sorts of odd jobs to keep their men busy: polish shoes, weapons, and all the equipment; fill sand-bags; keep the trenches in good repair; bring in supplies; help out in the field kitchen; even hold small drill practices. The most bizarre activity is catching rats. On some days, the area is crawling with them. They are as big as rabbits and so bold that they scurry across the backs of the men who are on guard duty. Rat catching becomes a game in which the men keep track of how many they catch. John is one of the favorite players; he spears the animals with his bayonet and grabs them with his bare hands when need be.

Yet the war remains a dirty business, with machine-gun fire and snipers who patiently lie in wait for their enemies. Each week there is usually someone who, because of the tedium and boredom, falls victim to his own absent-mindedness. And the frontline is long. Snipers weigh heavily on the morale of the troops. Even if it's relatively quiet, a small team must always be on the lookout, with weapons in hand. And a few shells land in their area nearly every day.

Suddenly gunshots are ringing out. John can hear the plop of their impact.

"Help, Mother! They got me!" he shouts from his post. Panicked, he feels the warm blood running over his face and down his neck. Thick red drops pour from his hands.

Everyone gets up and rushes toward him. Horrified, the men stay a couple of meters away.

"We were just talking, Walsh and I," John cries hysterically to the gathering soldiers, "about his girl who often writes to him . . ." He stares vacantly at the silent faces.

"My God! Didn't you hear that whizzbang coming?" Sergeant Kelly asks worriedly.

"We did," John sobs as he shakes the dark brown mud from his right sleeve. "Walsh pushed me against the wall for protection."

"Nasty shrapnel, Sergeant," mutters a corporal, squatting down to look.

John is just beginning to see the bloody torso lying at his feet. The head and arms are gone; Walsh is merely a lump of quivering, steaming flesh.

Everything is slowly spinning around John now. He sees a cap on the ground and the photo of the girl next to it. Thomas Carthy's voice sounds closer. Then John faints.

John and Tom talk about the incident during the following weeks. What is worse? To be hit by a piece of shrapnel that tears off a limb and rips open your belly? Or to be killed right away?

Most soldiers write letters during the four days of rest in De Brieke. Thomas Carthy seems like a true professional writer. Sometimes he scribbles ten letters a day for the dozens of illiterate men in the battalion.

"Oh, I could curse this war," Michael Mahoney exclaims. "Two whole weeks without a single letter from home!"

If the mail doesn't arrive on time, the Ypres Salient is full of soldiers with long faces and dragging feet.

"It's the postmen who will win the war," Tom declares, and he laughs.

"Then they should go on the offensive right away," Michael says earnestly.

"Shall I send something to Waterford for you, John?"

Tom asks.

"No, not right now, Tom. Thanks."

"That's what you always say."

"*I* will send greetings to Thomas's Avenue. All right?" Michael volunteers.

"I'd rather you didn't, Mike."

"Greetings from the one true *John* Condon, the hero of Wheelbarrow Lane," Michael teases.

"*No.* Lay off, I tell you!"

"Ohh! We'd best leave the children alone," Michael states. He is grumpy now as well.

John storms out the door. Tom approaches him a bit later.

"It would do you good to get a letter from home sometime, don't you think?" he begins. "Look . . ." He pulls an envelope from his breast pocket. "A photo of Mary in front of our cottage. *She* sends her greetings, at any rate."

"Thanks, Tom. It's sweet of her to think of me. Tell Mrs. Carthy I say hello to her, too."

"And Waterford—your mother, your sisters?"

John shrugs and turns his back to his friend.

"Do they have *any* idea at all that you're at the front, John?"

John clenches his teeth and runs away behind a shed where no one can see him.

APRIL 1915
BERLIN, GERMANY

Herr Doctor Haber and His Silent Killer

At the Kaiser Wilhelm Institute, the forty-seven-year-old director, Fritz Haber, bites his nails as he waits for news—a single telephone call that could change his life. Day and night he has toiled, not without danger, to write about the effects of new gas compounds. He has spent the best years of his life in the laboratory, spreading the renown of his scientific institute over Germany and the wide world. And spreading his own reputation, too, he must admit. *Surely those clever fellows on the Nobel*

Prize committee are acquainted with my work as a chemist, aren't they? Who knows, maybe someday . . . ? Professor Haber muses. Because he is a true *"Herr,"* a bit of vanity is not alien to him.

Those sixty-three thousand kilograms of gas-filled shells used against the Russians last winter were a fly in the ointment. His chemical gas compound appeared to be useless in the freezing cold. Those Cossacks had certainly inhaled it, but they unfortunately had lived to tell about it. An earlier attempt, in which the Germans used a kind of tear gas against the French and British in northern France, also fizzled out. That was in October. Those Frogs didn't even notice the gas, the swine!

It must *work this time,* Herr Haber frets. He is still fascinated by the first test, which he conducted safely behind glass. He recalls how that dirty brown stuff suddenly began to swirl when he broke open the ampoule—the hissing, effervescent dark green cloud; those thick chlorine fumes that remained suspended at a knee-high level above the floor in the test area. He remembers the dogs as they fell on their backs, howling in agony. The monkeys were like rubber balls bouncing against the ceiling. He *did* feel a little sorry for the horse. *But ach, so it goes in science,* the professor thinks, mollified. That old nag had already been blind from the previous chlorine gas test. At first the mare didn't react at all, because the cloud hovered under its belly.

"We need a bit of a draft," he had said to his assistant. "Just a light one."

"Shall I turn on the ventilator?" the fellow had suggested. "The exhaust system, perhaps?"

Fritz Haber can still picture the fumes spiraling up high. He sees the horse pull loose in panic, snort, cry, stretch its neck and cough, vomit, and finally spit blood until it falls over with a groan. The convulsions had lasted only three minutes. The test was a success.

The telephone on the desk rings.

"Hello? *Nein*, Schmidt. *Jetzt nicht*. This line must be kept open. I can't talk now. *Verstanden?*"

He puts the telephone receiver back and begins to pace up and down the dimly lit room. They *did* do everything properly, didn't they? Step by step, he walks through the drill practices, the same ones he had gone over countless times with the *Gaspioniers*, a secret army unit.

Dr. Haber hisses through his clenched teeth. *If all goes well*, he thinks . . .

APRIL 1915
WIELTJE, BELGIUM (NEAR YPRES)

Pee on Your Handkerchief

John and Tom roll up their thick winter jackets to the size of pillows.

"We can best put these warm things away until this evening, Tom."

"That bit of spring sun is wonderful. If the Fritzes were like us and wanted to enjoy some warmth, then maybe this war would be different," Tom says with a sigh. He looks for a dry spot on the long footboard that soldiers step up on as they emerge from the trench and run to the battlefield.

"Nothing to see across the way as usual, Mike?" John asks. His eyes are closed.

"Enjoy your rest," Michael Mahoney answers. "The Huns are sleeping."

"Tom, have you noticed those bright red buds? A few have already opened. Pretty, aren't they?" says John.

"They're poppies," Tom replies. "Soon you'll find them everywhere. Those little flowers are even blooming between the crosses of our comrades back there."

Generals are usually oblivious to poppies. John and Tom don't know that their relatively calm life at the front during the spring of 1915 is about to be disrupted by the plans of the German army command.

"We've sat in those trenches long enough," Commander-in-Chief Erich von Falkenhayn roars. "It is high time we reached the French harbors on the English Channel."

"Ypres must fall into our hands first," one of his stooges remarks dryly.

The other generals gathered around the table are silent. They know that capturing Ypres will be a bloodbath.

"Our new weapon, perhaps?" the same fawning voice asks.

The commander nods coolly. His lackey has played his role well. "*Meine Herren,* this is my proposal . . ."

His proposition almost sounds like a friendly question. But who would dare offend this top general by objecting to his plan?

At night, when French and British pilots are unable to spy, the Germans quietly work long and hard on their gruesome plan for Ypres. Special troops put five to six thousand steel canisters under the ground in the trenches. Each cylinder contains twenty to forty kilograms of compressed chlorine gas. The largest ones are two meters tall. Only the valves are visible above the clay. There is a rubber tube on each gas valve, ready to be laid over the parapet. The burrows in the earth will last more than a month. It's now just a matter of waiting for a light breeze from the right direction.

Early in the morning of April 22, 1915, the German cannons bombard the French and British-Canadian positions north of Ypres. Tom and John don't understand what has come over the enemy all of a sudden. They lie with their Irish battalion about two kilometers to the south on the defense bow. Shells and shrapnel keep raining down on them. The whole day they hear the booming of artillery and see smoke from the explosions rise up above the northern part of the Salient. Around five o'clock, it suddenly becomes dead still.

"Finally," Michael Mahoney pants.

"A person could get tired from all this," John says with a laugh.

"It's strange, though, that it's *so* quiet all of a sudden." Tom doesn't trust this entire business.

"There's nothing to see, just as always," Michael reports. "Maybe they've run out of shells!"

"Hey, Tom, Michael! Do you smell that?"

"Ugh . . . Bleach!" Michael calls.

"Are the Fritzes beginning their spring cleaning?" John jokes.

Tom doesn't understand what is happening, either.

"Shh. Be quiet," John demands. "Do you hear those voices?"

"It's the French," says Michael. "They're far away, but I can hear them shouting."

"It's coming from the Zouaves, if you ask me," Tom states.

"The Africans with their wide trousers and those flowerpots on their heads?" asks John.

"They're French colonial troops from Senegal," Tom explains.

"God, what could be the matter over there?" John wonders out loud.

"The shouts are coming from nearby now. From the Canadians, I think," Michael exclaims. "There's Sergeant Kelly."

"Something is going on with our neighbors, eh, Sergeant?" says Tom, the oldest in the group.

"I can't make much sense out of this, boys. The lieutenant with his periscope even less, for that matter. In the meantime, get ready. I've heard that reinforcements are coming."

For the first time in weeks, the men of the Second Battalion Royal Irish Regiment are lined up in row after row, ready to go over the top once again. John, Tom, Michael, and hundreds of others lean against the sandbags with their bayonets on their rifles and wait for the command to jump over the parapet.

"Now or never, Michael!" John says excitedly to his neighbor from Wheelbarrow Lane. They are standing way up in the first row.

Michael turns around to face Tom. "You look so pale," he says.

Tom is standing down on the foot plank in the overcrowded trench. Amid the jostling of elbows and shoulders, rifles and bags, he holds his cap in the air and wipes the beads of sweat from his forehead with his sleeve.

"Are you all right, Tom?" John asks, and he winks at Michael.

"It must be his age catching up with him, don't you think?" Michael whispers without looking back. "How old is our daddy, anyway?"

"Forty-seven. That makes a difference, eh? And how old are you? Nineteen, like my brother?"

"So we're the same age, eh, little one," Michael chuckles, and he winks.

"God, if those little boys in Ballybricken saw us now, how jealous they would be." John sighs.

"You mean your old friends?"

"Oh, O'Sullivan, Rogers, and that group of schoolgirls," he explains jokingly.

"Just listen to him," Michael says with a laugh. "Who's the schoolgirl here, Condon? I know O'Sullivan, at any rate. His older brother was in my class."

"School—Jesus, don't remind me!" John crows, and he suppresses a laugh. "Imagine, Mr. Baldwin here in Ypres!"

They burst out laughing. The men next to them can't understand why they're so cheerful. Their own nerves have reached the breaking point.

The big attack seems to have been canceled for that day. John and Michael are disappointed. Tom heaves a sigh of relief.

Little by little the next day, they hear about the unspeakable drama that played out for just a few short moments in the trenches a few kilometers farther up. From Steenstrate, the front lay open for hours over a breadth of six kilometers. African soldiers from the French colonies and *les pépères,* a division of older military men from Bretagne, didn't know what had hit them when the deadly chlorine gas cloud descended. Hundreds suffocated on the spot and died a silent, lonely death. More men fell dead in the skirmish immediately after the gas attack in hand-to-hand combat with the bayonets on their rifles. Whoever was still able to move fled to the bridge across the Canal Ypres-Yzer in Boezinge. Some didn't get that far—with burning lungs they jumped into the water. There were soldiers who remained on the ground for hours, spitting up blood. No one could help them.

The Germans seemed just as surprised by the effect of their new weapon. Only then did they realize that the way to Ypres was completely open and that the city was theirs for the taking. But there were no reserve troops to make the leap. When the Canadians launched a massive bloody counterattack in which they sacrificed hundreds of lives, the Germans succeeded in closing the breach. But by that time, it was too late for them to claim victory.

Less than a day later, at the crack of dawn on April 24, thousands of Canadians died near Sint-Juliaan in a second gas attack. Just as many would suffer permanent lung damage.

"What? Pee on our handkerchief?" each man asks himself out loud.

There is much laughter on the practice square in De Brieke.

Tom scratches under his cap. "Ever hear of such a thing?" he asks John and Michael.

"Could I use an old sock instead?" John inquires.

"*That* already stinks," Michael snorts.

"You can't hold *two* weapons at the same time and a handkerchief, too!" yells someone in a back row.

"Silence!" Sergeant-Major Larkin roars. He is the highest ranking noncommissioned officer of the company, and somewhat of a father figure to the battalion.

The other sergeants turn around and shout commands to their platoons. The men grow quiet.

"I repeat: pee on your handkerchief and hold it over your mouth. It's the only thing you can do to protect yourself against that goddamned gas when you're in the trench," Sergeant-Major Larkin calls sternly. "Colonel

Moriarty has urgently asked headquarters to send us real gas masks."

Various gas attacks follow during the next two weeks. John and his mates receive primitive masks for protection—cloths that have been saturated with a special liquid. When the men put these damp rags over their mouths and secure them with ribbon, they are scarcely able to breathe. The real gas masks are on the way, promises the colonel. Life in the trenches becomes depressing and grim. After all, you can't fight a gas cloud.

MAY 9, 1915

SINT-JULIAAN, BELGIUM (NEAR YPRES)

In the Mousetrap

At the beginning of May, the Second Battalion Royal Irish Regiment is finally ready to go over the top once again. The Irish occupy the first trench between the hamlet of Het Wieltje and the town of Sint-Juliaan. Next to them are the Royal Northumberland Fusiliers, the Fifth Battalion South Lancashire, the First King's Own, Second Essex, Second Royal Dublin Fusiliers, and on down the line.

"We must secure Mousetrap Farm and occupy it," Sergeant Kelly informs them.

"He means 'Shell Trap Farm,'" Tom whispers to John.

Everyone knows about the walled manor farm. It is a true magnet for shelling attacks because it is notated on every topographical map. Naturally, no one is going to be chomping at the bit to attack a farm called "Shell Trap." Therefore the place was renamed "Mousetrap," by orders from headquarters.

From the second firing line, the British continually lob shells over the ruins of the farm in the direction of Mauser Ridge, which lies behind it. Suddenly the field telephone rings a few steps from John. Michael nudges him.

"Here it comes," says John.

"Don't try to play the hero," Tom warns.

"You're nervous, aren't you?" John says with a laugh.

Tom is silent. The three watch Sergeant Kelly as he hands the receiver to Lieutenant Fottrell.

"Right, sir!" Fottrell exclaims curtly. He nods resolutely to Sergeant Kelly and looks at his wristwatch. No one has ever seen the lieutenant take his gun from the holster. The tension is nearly unbearable. The officer checks the little green cord dangling from his neck, which is attached to the butt of his revolver.

"Ready for attack, Sergeant?" he asks in a clear voice now. A forest of upright bayonets begins to move uneasily.

"Ready for attack!" Sergeant Kelly shouts through the passageway. His command is echoed by other sergeants farther up the trench. A red flare is fired above Mousetrap Farm. Someone blows a whistle in the distance.

"Go! Go! Go!" is resounding from all sides now. Before he realizes it, John is running amid a mass of shouting soldiers. A thick curtain of sulfur smoke reduces his visibility to just a couple of meters. He slows down and tries to get his bearings. The earsplitting explosions from shells drown out the clamoring of his comrades. With his head bowed and bayonet thrust forward, he walks between the bullets that are whistling past him. Nasty machine-gun fire is coming from the left. *The farm must be over there,* he thinks. At that moment there is a gigantic explosion. A sea of earth knocks him to the ground like a sledgehammer.

"Where am I?" John wipes the dust from his eyes and blinks in confusion at the bright blue sky above him.

"Quiet, John. Stay down," a familiar voice whispers.

But John struggles to sit up. Dazed, he finds himself on a pile of sandbags in the corner of a zigzagging trench. Filthy, mud-covered men walk back and forth as they drag limp bodies through the passageway. The sound of wailing is everywhere.

"Tom! What's happening?" John shakes the clay from his uniform. "Where is everyone?"

"Shh. We're safe here," Tom replies soothingly. "Our trench is just a little farther up—on that side, I think."

"Hey! Where's my rifle? And my cap?" John jumps up and looks around anxiously.

"I didn't look for them in all that mess on the battlefield." Tom sighs. "When I found you, I thought at first that you were dead as a doornail. There are *so* many wounded boys back there who were finished off with a bayonet. God, how frightened I was," he adds in a trembling voice. His head is between his knees.

"Did *you* bring me here?" John asks warily.

"Drag you here. Yes."

"And Mousetrap Farm? Did we take it?"

"John Condon!" Tom shouts angrily. "What the hell

do I care if we captured that pile of bricks? Today it's ours, tomorrow the Germans'. In God's name!" He storms around the corner.

"Tom! Tom, I'm sorry!" John calls, and follows him. His body feels completely knocked around. He finds Tom and stands with him.

"Stay calm," Tom orders in a fatherly way. "You've had darned good luck."

"Are we going to look for the others?"

"The others?"

"Yes. I want to know what Michael Mahoney thought of the attack."

Tom chooses his words carefully. "I'm afraid I haven't gotten through to you, John. Michael isn't the only one who fell today."

"Is he . . . ?"

Tom nods.

"How?"

"You don't want to know, John."

Michael Mahoney, John's neighbor from the same little alley in Waterford, is dead. No one will ever hear from him again. During these days, hundreds of name-less fellows disappear under the clay soil at Ypres, thousands of kilometers from home. Or they are smashed to a pulp by one of the countless shells.

At midnight on that same day, May 9, 1915, the German boys of the 234th Regiment are finally relieved after nineteen days and nights at the firing line. They have lost 1,463 men and 34 officers since the first gas attack on April 22. Their ranks have been depleted by two thirds.

During April and May 1915, the Second Battle of Ypres cost over 100,000 lives, on both sides. John Condon's battalion, the Second Battalion Royal Irish Regiment, which totaled about 800 men, was virtually wiped out. It was not the only Irish battalion in that campaign to suffer a great deal.

WHIT MONDAY

May 24, 1915
WIELTJE, BELGIUM

The Last Day

Midnight. The sky is full of stars. A forgotten church tower chimes in the distance.

"Father Gleeson's service was beautiful yesterday," Tom comments. "And on such a sunny Whit Sunday . . ."

They are silent. Tom and John are thinking about the same thing: the reading of names during the chaplain's sermon, the unbelievably long list of friends who are no longer with them.

"Masks on!" one man after another calls out through

the trenches. Yesterday, each soldier was given a pair of goggles as well as a mask for use against tear gas and chlorine gas.

At around one o'clock, Colonel Moriarty himself comes to warn his men. The troops who have just been relieved have smelled gas. It's likely due to technical problems of the German Gaspioniers. Each person puts on his primitive gas mask, a dirty, damp wad of cloth that fits over the mouth.

The machine gunners must wear their newly delivered hypo-helmets. The men look like ghosts in these thick flannel hoods with large mica windows. If a gas cloud comes, *they* certainly must hold their ground.

After the colonel and his entourage have left, most of the men remove their masks.

Three o'clock in the morning. The Germans launch three red flares into the sky from a hot-air balloon. For five seconds, the black, star-filled sky above the village of Poelkapelle turns into a bright red poppy. Then the heavens close up again, and the front is pitch-dark. John and his battalion are in the trenches near Wieltje, only two miles from Poelkapelle.

"In the name of God, what is happening now?" Tom whispers.

"Shh. Do you hear that?" says John.

The German trench that is closest to Mousetrap Farm is only 150 meters away. The hissing of hundreds of gas valves is very clear now.

"Gas!" ten voices call out at the same time, but the thick, poisonous clouds are already clinging to the ground nearby and rolling over the sandbag parapets. The first chlorine fumes wind their way into the British trenches. Men swear and walk over one another, tumbling over the footboard and kicking and thrashing in every direction. Helplessly they scratch their faces and necks to ribbons and purse their lips in search of air. Their death rattles are drowned out by the noise of the Irish machine-gun nests, which aim straight across the dark, swirling gas.

John feels his eyes starting to water. He squeezes them shut. His mouth mask is working fairly well. Tom is also withstanding the attack.

Glowing projectiles make a whining noise as they fly through the air and land several meters behind the men. Luckily the Irish are sitting deep in their trenches.

John and Tom shoot a few bullets in the direction of

the invisible enemy every now and then. The machine gunners receive the command to hold their fire. Rifle fire stops, as well. The sky gradually turns pale beyond the distant horizon. Everyone must now help lift the dead out of the passageways and roll them behind the trench. It is impossible to talk and complain through the masks. John's stomach lurches as he looks at all the contorted faces and ruptured eyeballs. He knows these dead soldiers very well, each and every one.

The wind picks up. The thick poison clouds have disappeared. More and more boys let their gas masks dangle around their necks. Suddenly they hear smaller explosions directly in front and up ahead to the right.

"Damn," Tom curses. "Those are hand grenades."

"Correct." A deep voice sighs behind them. It is Colonel Moriarty.

Soon it becomes dead still again. Then they hear clicking. John peeks through the top sandbags.

"There!" he whispers. "Colonel, sir, they're sneaking up on us." He is shocked by his own behavior, for ordinary soldiers are not allowed to speak to officers.

The battalion commander peers through the opening. "They're cutting through the barbed wire," he mutters.

"Do they think that we ran away because of the gas?" John asks Tom quietly.

"Or they think we've all suffocated," Tom mumbles back.

"Lieutenant!" It is the muffled voice of the colonel. "Hold your fire! Stay quiet—no one shoot."

The instructions are passed on immediately.

The shadows move closer at a slow, agonizing pace. The Irish wait anxiously for a command. Will they have to shoot or jump out of the trench? The mouse-gray uniforms of the German infantrymen now appear razor sharp in view. John notices the uncertain looks on their faces. *Ordinary boys, just like us,* he thinks. *They don't know what's in store . . .*

The Irish machine guns rip through the silence with a devilish rattle. The gray jackets become splattered with bright red blood. A large fellow jumps up and tries to throw a hand grenade but is riddled with bullets. Two seconds later, the grenade goes off with a dull crack, blowing him apart. The machine guns stop firing. A whistle shrieks through the passageway.

"Go, go! Go!" the sergeants yell.

John rushes forward with Tom behind him. The British storm ahead in broad rows, roaring like wild animals as they run toward the German side, where at least as many enemy soldiers are now brandishing their bayonets and yelling and shooting. Men to the right and left are falling down next to John, mortally wounded. It's impossible to recognize them in the turmoil. He fires again and again. Men are dropping in front of him, too. Dozens of Germans are lying in the barbed wire now.

John tries to find a hole in the barrier. "Colonel Moriarty!" he cries, startled to run into his leader.

With his pistol drawn, the high officer ducks through a narrow opening in the barricade and sinks to his knees. There is a large, round bloodstain on his back.

John hesitates.

"Leave him!" Tom shouts above the hellish din. "He's not going to make it."

The German voices that ring out are nearby and crystal clear. Suddenly, Tom and John are standing head to head with a small boy. The little German thrusts his bayonet forward and jumps. John fires. Everything is turning black . . .

Dead and (Twice) Buried

The sun is already shining high in the sky when John awakens, wide-eyed and frightened.

"Air . . . God, air! My throat is on fire. Aachh! Tom! I'm suffocating, Tom! Where are you? Bloody hell, answer me."

The clay earth and the thin, sparse grass surrounding his head have a pungent odor. He tries to turn on his side. "Aachh, my lungs are bursting . . . I'm going to puke . . . Gas, *gasss* . . . I've got to get away from here."

Screeching shells fly across the battlefield. John gasps for air. He tries to remember exactly what has happened. *But first open this jacket and breathe,* he thinks. *The collar is pinching me.*

His fingers are sticky from the clay. He struggles with the buttons. "Mama, help me!" he begins to whine in a high voice. "Mother! They got me, those Fritzes."

Big tears roll down his cheeks. Wheelbarrow Lane, Ballybricken, St. Patrick of the Holy Trinity Without, Rogers and O'Sullivan, Mollie and the baby, Fatso, Moira, his father . . . Everyone and everything flashes through his head.

John finally opens the top button. Then another. He clutches his chest. His shirt is clammy. He wrinkles his nose and looks at his fingers through half-closed eyes. "Bwaaah!" he cries. "All this blood is under my clothes! Tom! Help me, damn it."

Suddenly he opens his eyes wide and mumbles, "Holy Mary, what is that? My crotch is warm and wet. No . . . Have I peed in my pants? Air, fresh air—I can't breathe . . ."

He loses consciousness again.

John awakens, crying softly. He wants to get up, but his muscles refuse to move. He is unable to speak. It's dusky and cold. Someone has moved him. An unknown face studies him for a long time. John is turned on his side. Grass brushes against his feverish cheek. Someone is lying next to him. He feels a shoulder and sees a face nearby.

"Tom! T-T-Thomas Carthy!" he stammers. "Is . . . is that you, Tom?" He wants to talk, but his strength is gone. He shivers uncontrollably.

Why are you staring at the dark sky, Tom? he asks to himself wearily. *Answer me!*

"That boy wants to tell us something," says an unfamiliar voice high above him.

A man puts his ear to John's face. "Nineteen? Yes, that's it," he calls to someone far in the distance.

"No!" John groans angrily. He feels himself slipping away but wants to remain awake. He digs his nails into the grass.

"'Fourteen next month.' *That* is what he's saying!" the man calls out again.

John feels the ear brush against his dry lips.

"Fourteen. Not nineteen. Lies. Is that what he said?"

John is running through a long dark corridor. His feet are not touching the ground. Someone is standing in the white light far away, friendly and beckoning . . . At last.

ONE DAY LATER

May 25, 1915

GERMAN MILITARY HEADQUARTERS

BERLIN, GERMANY

New Strategies

The German chief of staff Erich von Falkenhayn is in a foul mood. The generals sitting around the table are curling their toes. Who will be the scapegoat today?

"*Meine Herren,* I've decided to call off the attack on Ypres for now."

The arrogant strategist nervously twirls the tips of his mustache. "On April twenty-second, our Gaspioneers surprised the enemy. The experiment was a success."

There are sighs of relief. But the tall, blond von

Falkenhayn stands up and continues in a trembling voice. "Alas, our officers missed their opportunity!" He examines the generals one by one.

"What has this Second Battle at Ypres procured? A few dozen square kilometers of ground! Nothing more. But yet . . ." he continues more quietly, "in one month at Ypres, we've knocked out an estimated sixty thousand of the enemy. British, Canadian, French, and Belgian troops, dead or wounded."

The generals nod approvingly.

"Alas," the commander says in a cold, careful voice, "we mourn the loss of thirty-five thousand of our own soldiers and officers. So it goes in war . . . They gave their lives *für Gott und Vaterland*."

Each man looks at the table in silence.

"For the time being, we'll hold our positions around Ypres just as they are. No more than that. We'll shift our offense to other fronts."

The commander takes his pointer and steps toward the map on the wall.

EIGHT YEARS LATER

July 25, 1923

OFFICE OF THE IMPERIAL WAR GRAVES COMMISSION

YPRES, BELGIUM

Ten in a Row

"Ten British soldiers, you say? Buried in a row? No false alarms, then?"

The old British serviceman Cleeve has the telephone pressed against his ear as he speaks to his assistant. "Tell me, Harris. I'll make a note of it."

There is crackling on the line. Cleeve scribbles down the message on a designated form. "So, along the Ypres-Zonnebeke railway," he repeats, "one kilometer from

Hellfire Corner? What? Yes, I know it well. By the grade crossing. Railway Wood is on the right. Take a left, toward Potijze. The mass grave lies just left of the road, a few meters from the railway bedding. Right by the monument of Captain Bowlby."

A half hour later, Cleeve parks his motorcycle with sidecar at the crossing. He stands straight as an arrow, as befitting a retired officer, and walks toward Harris and his two helpers. He greets them in his stuffy manner, well aware of his rank and class. "Good maawning!"

The gravediggers mumble something back while each quickly but politely grasps the visor of his cap with his thumb and finger. Cleeve begins to walk in a bow around the grave but doesn't get farther than halfway.

"Right." He nods curtly and reaches instinctively into his pocket, takes out a snow-white handkerchief and holds it over his nose. The gravediggers exchange amused glances.

"If you want to avoid the smell, it's better not to walk on that side, sir," Harris says, intentionally delaying this information. "The wind is coming from here, you see."

"Ten in a row," Cleeve exclaims with a stiff upper lip. He sighs, then walks back around the long pit and stands next to Harris.

"And reasonably well preserved, too, sir," his assistant adds.

"Most have been wrapped in a blanket, that's why," Cleeve mutters. "And then the clay, of course."

"Although they *are* beginning to stink rather awfully," Harris says, stating the obvious. "The sun and fresh air, you understand."

"Any identification possible, Harris?"

"I believe so, sir." He snickers, thinking about the mound of paperwork that awaits his boss.

"Numbers seven and eight seem a bit unusual," Harris continues. He jumps into the pit, straddles the seventh corpse, and unfolds the blankets around the two bodies.

"Two soldiers from the Royal Irish Regiment, sir. The uniforms are still easily recognizable. Besides, their chest straps are marked." He takes the belt from number seven, turns it over, and calls, "Soldier six-five-six-six!"

Cleeve begins to write diligently in his notebook. "We can identify him right away. And the other one?"

"Yes—the number is on his belt as well. It's even on one of his shoes. Number six-three-two-two."

"So, number eight in the row, soldier six-three-two-two," Cleeve says aloud, writing it down.

"Sir? You noticed, as well?" Harris asks a bit hesitantly. "You noticed that they're lying very close to each other?"

"This one was very young." Cleeve points to number eight. "No longer a child, but . . ."

"Not yet a man, eh?"

Cleeve nods.

"And the other one could have been his father." Harris sighs.

Three days later, Cleeve signs the last exhumation report with a flourish. *Two weeks' vacation at last*, he thinks. *Tomorrow morning I'm on the first train out of Ypres, and then I'll catch the ferry from Oostende to Dover and spend a few days with the family.*

He licks the brown envelope closed and files the duplicate copies in a thick ring binder. His eyes focus on the top sheet. *Private 6566 T. Carthy, 47y., Clonmel (Ire.), and Private 6322 J. Condon, presumed 14y., Waterford (Ire.). Both 2BnRIR. Both missing (dead) since 5/24/1915. Now buried next to each other in plot LVI, row F, Poelkapelle, British Cemetery, in Flanders, Belgium.*

"A rather strange case," he mumbles to himself. He closes the binder and sets it in on the rack. He glances at the clock. Five minutes to six.

"I have a few moments yet." Cleeve sighs. An English newspaper is spread open on the large table. He decides to kill time by reading for a bit. A small article catches his attention: NOBEL PRIZE WINNER DOCTOR FRITZ HABER TO BE THE GUEST . . .

SOME WORDS FROM THE AUTHOR

Who was Fritz Haber?

Fritz Haber (1868–1934) was a German chemist who developed chlorine gas (1915) and mustard gas (1917) for use in warfare. In 1918, Haber received the Nobel Prize in chemistry, not for creating these deadly gases but for other work, primarily for what became known as "the Haber-Bosch process," in which nitrogen and hydrogen are combined to form ammonia. This method is critical for the manufacturing of artificial fertilizer, and was responsible for vastly improving agriculture all over the world. Because nitrates are a key component in explosives, the process also boosted Germany's munitions production during World War I.

Haber's wife, a brilliant chemist in her own right, was horrified by her husband's work with poison gas. She committed suicide while Haber was supervising the first gas attack at Ypres. Apparently he put the war before his family, for he did not even attend her funeral.

Haber felt a great sense of patriotism toward his country. When the war ended and Germany was forced to pay huge reparations, he wanted to contribute to the costs. For years he tried to extract gold from seawater, but his efforts were to no avail.

Was John Condon really fourteen years old?

Yes, I strongly believe that John Condon was, at the time of his death, fourteen years old. You can find the Condon family of Thomas's Avenue, Waterford, Ireland, in the 1901 and 1911 censuses. If you presume that the brothers Patrick and John made a deal and swapped their names, then "age fourteen" matches. These documents may not always have been filled in with 100 percent accuracy by the local policemen. How can nonbelievers explain that this story of John's being fourteen was so well known shortly after the war? That the Waterford boy was the talk of the town for many years? Why did newspapers go on repeating this story ever since World War I? The fact that he was eighteen on his enlistment, which can be found in the army archives, does not prove his real age. Of course he had to pretend he was old enough to enlist.

There is also a document stating that Patrick Condon died in 1940. Someone changed his age there: forty-two was crossed out, and replaced by thirty-nine. There must have been some confusion there. Were they still afraid to reveal his real age, maybe fearing the loss of a pension or other consequences?

There are still some loose ends to the John and Patrick Condon story. There are strong indications that Patrick Condon, using his older brother John's name, ran away from his Irish hometown of Waterford to Liverpool, England, before he went to the front. I did not know these facts when I wrote the original novel (in Dutch, published in Belgium). On July 7, 1938, the *Waterford News* published an article entitled "Ran Away to Great War. Waterford Youth Who Was Killed at Age of Fourteen. Boyish Adventure. Hid in Ship, Pretended He Was Eighteen." The author interviewed Nicholas Condon, Patrick's cousin and inseparable playmate. They were so attached that they were called the Condon twins. Nicholas shares the following: "Patrick was thirteen at the end of 1914. I was a few years older. On a sudden impulse we got on board of the *Clodagh,* a small steamer which plied between Waterford and Liverpool." The two stowaways arrived at their uncle's in Salford. The uncle offered to help them find work, but there were so many young men in uniform passing to and fro that they joined the army. Nicholas says they both enlisted with the Lancashire Fusiliers, later to be posted with the East Lancashires. Says Nicholas, "Patrick was a strapping lad for his age. They asked no questions when he said he was eighteen. But my cousin wasn't satisfied. He wanted to join the Royal Irish Regiment. This was our first and last separation. We never saw each other again. I came through the war all right. But my cousin was killed by a bursting shell. He could only have seen a few months' fighting."

A few years ago, in 2003, I met John Condon, son of Patrick. He was an elderly man, and together with his cousin Sonny he visited the grave of his uncle "John" in Belgium. They were the first of the Waterford Condons ever to visit the grave of their relative John Condon, who died in 1915. Talking to them reassured me that

"John" really was a kid when he was killed in Flanders Fields. They were very convinced. And did they know anything about the identity swap? No challenge arose at all when I gave them my interpretation of "John" being in fact his younger brother Patrick. But they also preferred not to elaborate on that issue. Does it still remain a half secret among the family members?

Is it John Condon's grave?

Some say that the body in John Condon's grave is not his but that of the rifleman Patrick Fitzsimmons, and that there has been a misidentification. John Condon and Patrick Fitzsimmons had the same service number: 6322. John belonged to the Second Battalion Royal Irish Regiment (RIR), while Patrick was one of the Second Battalion Royal Irish Rifles (also RIR). No one can exclude a misidentification, and only a DNA test would prove right or wrong.

But no one can doubt that there once was a Waterford boy who dreamed of adventure and glory. There was nothing he wanted more than to become a soldier. He went off to war in France and Belgium, but he never returned to Ireland. His body rests under a headstone somewhere in Flanders Fields.

This novel is not just a true story about a boy soldier who lived almost a century ago. Let's not forget that UNICEF estimates that there are some 250,000 child soldiers in the world now, mainly in Africa.